ONE PERFECT LOVE

SEQUEL TO ONE SMALL VICTORY

MARYANN MILLER

To my friend, Becky Wheeler-Pickett. She knows all the reasons why.

ONE

JENNY KNELT in front of the small headstone, reaching out with one finger to lightly trace the inscription — *Michael Jasik 1996 – 2014 – Beloved Son.* It had been two years since the funeral, but there were times she forgot it wasn't just yesterday. Those were days when the grief snuck up behind her and then slammed her in the gut like a battering ram. Those were the days when she was a total wreck. Unable to work. Unable to do much of anything except maybe breathe.

And even that was a challenge.

She didn't know why she kept coming here. She knew Michael wasn't here. At least not in spirit. According to the preachers of her childhood, Michael was either in heaven or hell. There was no in-between with those men who spoke of a God who would rain fire and brimstone down upon the sinners of this world. Jenny always had a hard time relating to a God like that. Perhaps that's why she stopped going to church as soon as she could move away from home and escape the mandate that "you will go to church as long as you live in my house."

Even though she never acknowledged it, a small part of her did know exactly why she came here so often. Besides the officers at the Little Oak police department, Michael was the only one who knew that Jenny had shot a man two years ago.

Her grief was split between the loss of a son and the loss of a piece of herself.

She could share that with Michael.

She had also been able to share that with Steve. Warm, wonderful, wise Steve who had been the first man since Ralph that she had even considered as someone who could be a permanent fixture in her life. The chemistry was there. They both recognized it as they'd worked together on that drug task force. Then, it had been professional boundaries that kept them on either side of a distinct line. Afterward, they had tried to build something, but they both just found it too hard to try to be normal when nothing was normal in either of their lives. So she had gone back to being a single woman without a relationship.

Most days, that was tolerable. She had her kids. And her friends. And her work. And her wonderful business partner. But it had been a long time since she had a companion, in bed and otherwise. That one person you would call first with good news, or bad, who was not your girlfriend. And someone to hold close in bed on cold winter nights.

A cool October breeze brushed across her face, drying the tears that had run down her cheeks in a great warm river. This was a safe place to let the tears pour out. She couldn't do that at home in front of her other kids. They were dealing with mountains of grief in their own way. She knew that, and if they still cried, they hid it well. Not like the first year when tears cluttered the house like old newspapers and magazines that should have been thrown out months ago. The crying couldn't continue indefinitely. She realized that, so she had started hiding her tears, trying to establish a different kind of normal that didn't include losing emotional control at odd moments in time.

This fall, Scott had run headlong into his senior year, and Jenny didn't want to be all emotionally needy when he was focused on school and grades and to which college he would apply. And Alicia? Well, Alicia was still being the strong little girl she'd been most of her life, holding them together as a family the best she could. Even though she was now thirteen and blossoming into a lovely young lady, she would always be Jenny's little girl. And she would always be the strong one. The peacemaker. The one who encouraged smiles, not tears.

Jenny rose, checking her watch. Almost eight. Scott and Alicia were on their way to school by now. Earlier, she'd left them finishing breakfast with stern orders to clean up when they were finished. They didn't ask why she was going to work so early. Some things none of them asked about. It was still an hour before opening, but she knew she should be headed to the shop by now. Her partner Mitchell was coming in late, so she was going to be on her own for most of the morning. He was taking Jeffrey to a doctor appointment. That horrible AIDS just might claim another victim. Poor Jeffrey. Poor Mitchell.

After one more glance at the headstone, Jenny turned and hurried to her car. Luckily, she was only a few miles from the floral shop she'd owned with Mitchell for ten years now. It was housed in an old, Victorian-style house that she'd recently painted a soft blue. It had needed paint for several years, but, well, life had interfered, starting with Michael's death. Shortly after he was killed in that car accident, she'd muscled her way on to a drug task force to help the police stop the proliferation of drugs in the sleepy little town of Little Oak.

Until remnants of a white powdery substance had been found at the scene of the accident that had claimed her son's life, she'd had no idea that the use of cocaine was so prevalent in the town. She was too busy raising three kids by herself and trying to run a business. Then the accident. Then the awareness. Then the task force. She still couldn't believe she'd done it. When she'd joined the task force, she was numb with grief and not thinking well at all, a fact of which her mother and her best friend kept reminding her. But she'd persevered, passed the physical and helped bring down the main drug supplier for North Texas.

Pulling to a stop in front of her shop, Jenny glanced at the sign and smiled. A TOUCH OF JOY/Flowers for all Occasions. She'd thought about changing the sign when she painted the building, but Mitchell had vetoed that idea. He'd reminded her of why she'd named it that in the first place. "Flowers bring joy no matter the circumstances."

He was right. Flowers helped celebrate the happy occasions and brought comfort in the not-so-happy occasions.

She locked her car and hurried up the walk, stopping short when she noticed the front door was slightly ajar. *What the ...?* Her heart thumped so hard against her ribs, she thought it would bust right out. She took a breath and pushed the door open, calling out, "Mitchell? You here?"

Silence.

Taking a tentative step inside, she paused a moment to let her eyes adjust to the dim interior, then she saw it. The mess. The arrangement she always kept on the end of the front counter now on the floor, flowers scattered and squashed. The vase smashed to pieces. Papers strewn about, some floating in the water from the arrangement. The old grandfather clock pushed over. Chairs upended. Her cash box tossed into the corner. Open. Empty. Anger and frustration warred within her, fighting for top billing. Some horrible person had broken in and done all this.

4

Was that someone still here?

That question sent her heart racing again, so fast she thought it might explode right out of her chest. She tried to take a breath to steady herself, standing absolutely still for a moment. Then she shook the fear aside and pulled a can of Mace from her purse. She held her hand out as she stepped the rest of the way inside, careful to avoid the part of the flooring in the entry that always squeaked. She'd never fixed the loose board because it always alerted her to a customer if she was in the back design area. Letting the can of Mace lead the way, she walked slowly around the front counter to the doorway that led to the back of the shop. She sidled up to one side, peeking around the corner. What was she thinking? Clearing the building like some cop on a TV show? She smothered a laugh, knowing the impulse was driven by manic fear, not humor.

The design part of the shop was one spacious room with wide work counters on two walls, refrigerators on another, and shelving on the fourth. It, too, was a mess, but there was no place for an intruder to hide. She took a deep breath to stop the pounding of her heart, dropped the Mace back into her purse, and pulled out her cell to dial 911.

———

Lieutenant Steve Morrity looked up as Officer Linda Winfield poked her head into his office. "Just took this call from dispatch," she said. "Thought you might want to respond."

"What is it?"

"Burglary."

"Why aren't you taking it?" Being his subordinate, she was the most likely person to handle a burglary, but rank was just a title here, not a pecking order. The whole department was comprised of Chief Gonzales, Steve, Linda, and four patrol officers. They tended to work together more on equal footing than not, and Steve liked it that way. Still, he had that murder case wrapping up with tons of paperwork and didn't need anything else right now. Linda knew that.

She walked over and dropped a piece of paper on his desk. It fluttered for a moment in the breeze from the overhead fan, then settled on the burnished wood. "Thought you might want an excuse to see this woman again."

"Huh?"

"Read the name and address."

Steve picked up the paper and read the information. Jenny? Really? My Jenny? Steve shook his head. How absurd to even think that. She wasn't his Jenny. Not that he hadn't wanted her to be when they worked together on that drug case. They both had recognized the electricity that sizzled between them, and they'd tried to act on it once the case was over. But she needed to back off. She needed time, and he'd understood. Hell, at the time, he'd still needed to back off. He'd known he wasn't over losing Katie. Not enough to fully allow another woman into his heart. And Jenny deserved a man who was able to give her his all.

Now?

He smiled. It was possible that he was ready. Was she?

Linda chuckled. "I was right."

Steve had almost forgotten Linda was still there until the laugh. He looked up at her. "What do you mean?"

"I'm surprised you do so well at poker."

Now Steve chuckled. "Get out of here."

Linda stepped out, and Steve shut down his computer after saving the report he'd been working on. He wasn't surprised that Linda had remembered about Jenny. Steve had talked enough about her that Linda, ever the romantic, had urged Steve to say *screw policy*. Linda knew that while Steve was willing to skirt around some things in the policy handbook, keeping a professional boundary between himself and a CI was one he took seriously.

Steve shook the memories off, stood, grabbed his jacket, and headed out. He didn't need the paper with the address. He knew where to find Jenny.

A short drive later, Steve pulled the unmarked car to a stop in front of the flower shop and turned off the engine, noting that not much had changed about the old building, except for a new paint job. Before he even got to the door, it opened, and Jenny was standing there. She had changed a lot in the time since he'd last seen her. The tight lines of grief and anxiety around her eyes were less noticeable. Her hair was cut in a short straight bob, dark brown hair framing her face, and she absolutely took his breath away. He grimaced inwardly at that thought. That kind of stuff was for a romance novel. Not that he read romance novels. But Linda devoured them, and when things were particularly slow at the station, she'd feel compelled to share a particularly juicy passage with him in the break room. Men were always having their breath taken away, or feeling their hearts stopping, and other physical reactions that always made him blush. She seemed to like to make him blush.

And Jenny apparently liked to see the blush as well. He hadn't even been aware of the red heat creeping up his neck until she said, "Getting a lot of sun lately?"

For a moment he was puzzled, then he laughed and said, "No, not so much."

"I'm surprised to see you."

"You called."

She hesitated a moment as if processing that, then said, "Right." She opened the door. "I was expecting a patrol officer."

"They were all busy." He smiled, and then followed her

inside, thinking how nice it was to fall back into that friendly banter they'd shared when they'd worked together.

Once Steve surveyed the rooms, careful not to touch anything, he called back to the station to have Linda come out with a couple of patrol officers to dust for prints, take pictures, gather any evidence, and document the crime scene. Linda had taken the CSI training in Dallas, so she could take care of the preliminary crime scene analysis.

Steve closed his notebook where he'd written down Jenny's statement, covering the details of her actions from the time she'd arrived. He'd frowned when she told him about going into the shop. "You should have stayed outside and called us."

"I'm not exactly helpless, you know."

There was a meaning behind her words that reminded them both of those months when she'd worked on the drug task force.

"I know." He smiled. "I'd ask if you want to help us with this one. But I'm afraid you'd say yes."

Jenny smiled in return.

Now they were standing outside the shop, and Jenny asked, "Do you think this could be related to what I did before?"

Steve thought for a moment then shook his head. "The whole drug scene has been pretty quiet around here. And if anyone wanted to retaliate against you, they would've done it right after that business."

"So this is random?"

"Maybe. There've been a couple of other burglaries downtown. Might be the same person. Or persons."

Now, despite the earlier banter, a hint of awkwardness hung between them like a piece of gauze, and they looked at each other for a long, silent moment. It was as if once the business was taken care of, neither of them knew what to say.

Steve shifted his weight from one foot to the other and said, "I'd better get back to the station."

"Oh. Sure. You must be busy. I'll wait outside until Linda gets here."

Steve nodded. "Good idea."

Mentally kicking himself for not moving the conversation from professional to personal, Steve strode to the car. *Real slick move, there.*

———

Jenny watched Steve as he went down the front walk, looking ever so good in his blue jeans, tightly cinched around his slim waist. She recalled that wonderful evening they'd had at Billy Bob's in Fort Worth two years ago. It started as just a place to meet to trade information. Since everyone knew everything about everyone else in a small town, it had been necessary for them to meet far away from Little Oak and prying eyes.

That night had turned into more than a meeting when Steve had suggested they dance. "To keep up appearances," he'd said. "Don't want people wondering why we're here."

That had been a ruse, Jenny knew. The look that had accompanied the statement had told her that. Still, she'd acquiesced and joined him on the dance floor, where he held her close during a slow song, their bodies fitting together as though they had always danced.

And today she had to admit that she still had feelings for Steve. Her heart had beat a little faster when she'd seen him pull up in front of the shop earlier, and his smile of greeting had been as good as a comforting caress.

And today she needed a caress. Her emotions were being tossed around like an out-of-control carnival ride. She was still so angry at the break-in. The violation of it all. How dare somebody do that? Steal? Trash a place? She knew it happened time and again to businesses all over the world, but this was her world. Her business. And whoever it had been should have to pay. Big time.

When a black and white patrol car pulled up to the curb, Jenny shook those thoughts aside and greeted Linda. She had two other officers with her, and the crew went inside and started to work, scattering black dust on surfaces for prints and snapping pictures.

Jenny stayed out of the way while the officers worked, and after they left, she stood looking at the mess that the intruder had left in the design area. Flowers strewn everywhere. Vases broken, the shards of glass scattered across the hard cement floor, glittering in the overhead light. Ribbons had been shredded. Moss strewn everywhere. All of this just for a few hundred dollars that Jenny kept in the cash box. The drawer under the front counter where she normally kept the box had been locked, but any enterprising burglar could easily spring that lock. A fact that both Steve and Linda had pointed out when they'd looked at the drawer.

Fighting down another surge of anger, Jenny opened the first of the two large refrigerators that housed flowers waiting to be made into gifts. Thankfully, about half of the flowers were intact, so they could manage the orders that had to go out later today. God. How could she just start working as if this was a normal day? But she had to. And she needed help cleaning up if she had any hope of getting said orders made. She pulled out her cellphone and called her friend, Carol. When Jenny told Carol what happened, her friend shrieked, "Oh my God. Were you there? Are you hurt?"

"No to both questions, Carol. Somebody must have broken in early this morning because the place was a mess when I got here at eight."

It was good to talk to her best friend again. It had taken almost a year for Carol to get over George. To get over the fact that Jenny was responsible for George going to jail. That Jenny was responsible for destroying what Carol thought was the best thing that had ever happened to her in years. She'd lost her first husband to cancer and hadn't filled her heart or home since.

Luckily, Carol had finally come to realize that George was not the best thing to happen to her. A drug dealer was never a good thing for anyone, and so, a few months later, she'd forgiven Jenny for her part in the whole ugly mess.

"What can I do?" Carol asked. "Do you need help cleaning up?"

"That would be great. Mitchell's coming in a bit later, and he can do some of the heavy lifting. But there's plenty of other stuff we can do."

"Heavy lifting? You could do the heavy lifting." Carol laughed and Jenny joined in, surprised she could laugh about something as horrible as having been invaded this way, but maybe she needed the laughter to smother her frustration and anger.

TWO

ON THE WAY back to the station, Steve stopped at McDonald's for a burger. Not his burger of choice. That came from Randy's Steakhouse. The burgers there were made fresh, pattied out from bulk ground beef, but it was not a place to go to if you were in a hurry. He ate quickly, washing the sandwich down with iced tea, and got back in his car. Fifteen minutes later, he was at his desk, finishing the paperwork for that murder case.

Nasty one.

When the rodeo queen had been found dead four months ago, it had appeared to be a simple case. The boyfriend was angry because she'd broken up with him. The way she'd been killed, gutted like a deer in hunting season, Steve had figured the boyfriend did it. Most murders, unless it was gang or drug-related, came down to someone close to the vic. But this one took a dangerous turn when another girl was killed. Same MO: raped and belly cut open. When he'd seen her, Steve was angry like he hadn't been in a long time. A real nasty SOB was responsible for this.

Turned out Steve was right about that. A serial killer had stopped in their town on more than one occasion, staying long enough to find some young girl to eviscerate. The killer was a trucker who would stay at the old, seedy motel at the edge of town. When a witness, who had seen the girl with an older man at the motel, came forward, Steve had gone to check it out, thinking at first that it would be a routine inquiry.

He was wrong.

In room 221, Steve found a tall, bulky man with a stubble of beard who seemed to sense that Steve was police the minute he saw him. Alarm had flashed in the man's eyes, and he'd stepped back, slamming the door. When Steve kicked the door open, the man had come at him with a knife, and the cut under Steve's ribs reminded him of how close the man had come to gutting him. What saved Steve was his speed and agility. The man was like a bear just out of hibernation. Nasty and mean and threatening, but slow and awkward. Steve had slipped to one side, eluding the second swipe of the knife and leveling his Glock at the man. He shot him in the shoulder, but the man kept coming, so Steve had brought him down.

That had been just a week ago, and Steve still had the stitches in his side – ten of them – and a dressing he had to change every day. He also still had to finish the incident report, which was standard procedure when an officer fires his weapon.

Late that afternoon, Linda came into Steve's office with some preliminary reports from forensics on the burglary at Jenny's shop. "We got a good print, but so far nothing is showing up in any databases."

"Checked them all already?"

"Still waiting for IAFIS. But nothing from the military or local police." Linda took a seat in the visitor chair in front of his desk. "So?"

Steve frowned. "So, what?"

"Did you ask her out?"

It took just a second for Steve to realize what Linda meant. He shook his head.

"Why not? What the hell are you waiting for?"

Steve shrugged. "I panicked."

"Panicked? You? Big, tough police officer who just took down a nasty serial killer?"

"That's different."

Linda laughed, then turned serious. "Yeah. I guess it is."

She stood and walked to the door, then turned back. "My advice. Don't let her get away again."

"Yeah, yeah, yeah." Steve motioned for her to leave, and she did.

Now he couldn't concentrate on the forms he was filling out. Thoughts of Jenny kept intruding, and he kicked himself for running away like that this morning. That's what he'd done. Run like a scared hound when things had gotten awkward between them on the steps to her shop.

Well, he wasn't going to run anymore.

———

Mitchell rushed into the shop and grabbed Jenny in a tight bear hug. She struggled against him. "Put me down. You're breaking my ribs."

Mitchell released her, and she asked, "How's Jeffrey?"

"He's fine. How are you?" Mitchell looked around. "Oh my God, Jenny. Look at this place. Are you okay?"

"Settle down, Mitchell. One question at a time. I'm fine. Nobody was here when I got here, so nobody could hurt me."

"Did you call the police?"

"Of course I called the police. They've been here already. They did all the crime scene stuff, and now we just have to clean up. Carol's in the back."

Carol had come an hour earlier, and the two of them had worked to put the design area in order. Now Carol was mopping up water that had been spilled in the back while Jenny worked on the mess in the front.

Mitchell leaned over to pick up a crushed purple iris and fingered the limp, bruised petals. "Who could have done this?" He looked at Jenny, and she was sure he was holding back tears. "The poor flowers."

Now she knew he was holding back tears. He loved the flowers almost as much as he loved people. Well, some people. And for sure as much as he loved the little bulldog he and Jeffrey had rescued last year. "I know," Jenny said. "I don't know why whoever did this had to be so destructive. They tore up the design room, too. And there was nothing in there to steal."

Jenny started pulling papers out of the puddle of water, then looked up at Mitchell, who was still holding the wilted flower. "Why don't you go on and start on the orders that need to be done today?"

"Okay."

Jenny finished cleaning up the front area and then went into the back to help Mitchell with the flower arrangements. It was a good thing that they only had ten orders. There was no way they could have filled any more than that on such a horrible day. Carol got them all a late lunch from the little downtown deli that served great sub sandwiches. After they all ate, Carol left them and went home.

At six, the floral arrangements were all made and loaded into Mitchell's van for delivery. Jenny dragged her weary body home to find two kids waiting for dinner. She didn't have the energy to cook, so she pulled a pan of lasagna out of the freezer and put it in the oven. She talked Scott into making a salad and Alicia into fixing drinks and setting the table. While they prepared dinner, she told the kids what had happened.

"Oh my gosh," Alicia said. "Are you okay, Mom?"

As much as Jenny appreciated the concern, she was really getting tired of that first question to come out of everyone's mouth. As if she couldn't take care of herself. Hadn't she proved anything two years ago? But she smiled and allowed Alicia her concerns. "I'm fine," Jenny said. "Nobody was hurt. Nothing was hurt. Except a few flowers, and you know how Mitchell feels about the flowers."

Alicia laughed then said, "Yes. He thinks they're alive."

"They are alive."

"I know, Mom, but you know what I mean." Alicia put the glasses of water on the table.

"Yes, I do." For a moment Jenny pictured Mitchell standing at the shop, cradling that crushed flower. She'd known he was the perfect partner for her business when he'd come in for the interview ten years ago, holding a bouquet of flowers in much the same loving manner.

"So," Scott said, pulling the lasagna out of the oven and setting it on hot pads on the table. "Did you call the police?"

Another repeated question Jenny wished she didn't have to hear. Did everyone think she was a numbskull? "Of course I did."

"Any particular police?"

Jenny glanced up to see a little smile on Scott's face. "What do you mean?"

Scott scooped a large helping of lasagna onto his plate, and then said, "You know what I mean."

Jenny wondered about that for a moment. Could he really mean Steve? Other than running into him at the city Fourth of July picnic this past summer, none of them had seen Steve since ... She let the thought slide away as Scott winked at her. She laughed and delayed her response by scooping lasagna onto a plate for Alicia, before filling one for herself. Then she looked at Scott and said, "As a matter of fact, Steve did come out."

"Steve?" Alicia cried in that way only a teenage girl can. "As in? You know, the hunky police guy you work with?"

Jenny let out a deep breath. "Yes, Alicia. The very attractive police guy I *worked* with. Past tense. Now, will you both stop with all the questions and eat your supper?"

The kids complied, eating in silence, but Jenny noted the looks that traveled between them. And later, when all the dishes were cleared, and the kids were in their rooms working on their homework, Jenny wondered about how Steve had stayed so prominent in their minds for so long. The few times they'd dated almost two years ago, she had been careful not to indicate to the kids that this was going to be anything permanent, which turned out to be a good thing when both she and Steve realized that neither one of them was ready for a relationship. But had the kids started to form a bond anyway? Could that have happened in just the few times they were all together before Jenny put the brakes on?

Considering the questions, Jenny sipped the coffee she'd brought into the living room with her. There was no doubt that the kids needed a man in their life. Even at this almost too-late date when they were both teens, one ready to leave hearth and home for college and the other looking ahead to high school.

To his credit, Ralph, her ex, was being a better father than he'd been the first years after the divorce. Actually, better than the last few years of the marriage as well. Michael's death had shaken him to his roots, and it was a shame that it had taken something so devastating to wake him up. Still, while she was grateful that Ralph visited when he could and called the kids frequently, he was still too many miles away. His job was in California, where he devoted too many hours to maintaining databases. The kids visited him every summer for a couple of weeks, and last year they'd spent the Christmas holidays out there with him. But that still wasn't as good as having a man around on a more frequent basis for all those things a mom was not good at. And if she admitted it to herself, Jenny would say that she wouldn't mind having someone to wake up with every morning. Not to mention those luscious nights she could only vaguely recollect due to recent years of unwilling chastity.

A knock on the front door interrupted Jenny's thoughts. She put her coffee cup down and hurried over, opening the door to see Steve standing on the porch. Had she willed him here by just thinking about him? "This is a surprise," she said, mentally scrambling to push the remnants of the luscious-nights thoughts out of her mind. "Uh...do you have something to report?"

"No." He appeared to be feeling as awkward as she was, shifting slightly from foot to foot. "Just stopped by to check on you. I was so busy being official earlier I didn't even think to ask how you were feeling about it all."

She offered a small smile. "I'm okay."

He studied her for a moment then asked, "Are you sure?"

She started to nod, but then the dam that she'd built around herself cracked and all the emotions from the day started to flow out with the warm tears that ran down her cheeks. She wasn't okay. She'd been robbed. She'd been violated. And all day she'd pretended she was strong enough to just treat it like a minor inconvenience.

And here she was crying in her front foyer like a baby.

Steve stepped into the open doorway and touched her on the shoulder. "Oh, Jen. I didn't mean to make you cry."

The moment, his presence, his kindness was so much like that first day he'd come over unofficially two years ago it broke the rest of her defenses. She leaned into his broad chest and took comfort in the warmth of his arms around her. The thump of his heart increased in tempo, and she remembered that sound, too. It was a prelude to something more than comfort, and her body responded to the memory. And the need. She was about to lift her face when Alicia gave a whoop and bounded down the stairs. "Steve!"

"We'll talk about this later," Steve whispered in Jenny's ear.

"Talk about what?"

"You know." His lips touched her neck just below her ear. There was no doubt what he meant, and Jenny felt a tingle of anticipation as she brushed the moisture off her cheeks. She stepped back so Steve could come all the way into the house, and Alicia ran over to give him a big hug.

When Alicia let go, the three of them stood there in an awkward silence for a moment, none of them seeming to know what to say or what to do, then Steve made a move to the door. "I should go. Let you get to your dinner."

"We're finished," Jenny said.

Silence reigned again for a moment, then Alicia smiled at Steve. "Stay for dessert," she said, then turned to her mother. "We have dessert. Don't we?"

"We do. Unless you kids ate the rest of the pie Grandma brought over yesterday."

"It's still here." Alicia ran toward the kitchen. "I'll serve."

Steve didn't move. "I shouldn't intrude."

"It's okay," Jenny said, taking his arm. As they passed the staircase, Jenny called out, "Scott? Want some pie?"

A few seconds later, Scott came bounding down the stairs,

taking them two at a time, making Jenny's heart jump. She hated when he did that, always dreading the day he might trip and fall and break his neck. "Slow down," she said.

Scott grinned when he saw Steve and walked over to shake his hand. "We were just talking about you."

"You were?" Steve looked from the teen to Jenny.

"I told them about calling you after the break in." Jenny hoped the warmth on her cheeks didn't show up in glaring red. She hurried into the kitchen where Alicia was already cutting the half a pie into four equal pieces. "Scott," Jenny called over her shoulder. "Check the freezer for ice cream. I think there's some vanilla bean left."

Scott found the ice cream and added a generous scoop to each piece of pie. Jenny made coffee for her and Steve, then they all sat down and started to eat. It was such a normal, family thing to do Jenny's heart jumped again, but this time a different emotion triggered the response. This was pure contentment, and she knew her earlier musings about Steve and the kids were right. The kids needed him. Did he need them?

Scott finished his pie and pushed the plate aside. "Catch the burglar yet?" he asked Steve.

Steve shook his head. "Takes time. More than a day for sure."

"Maybe Mom can help you again," Alicia said.

Jenny drew in a deep breath, and Steve laughed. "We already discussed it."

"And?" Alicia prompted into his silence.

"It can't possibly happen," Jenny said. "What I did before. That was a one-time thing."

"Then how will you see Steve again?"

Jenny drew in a breath again, wishing her kids weren't so

outspoken and hoping that Steve wouldn't see the statements as a push toward something he might not want.

"That's a very good question, darlin'." Steve spoke to Alicia, but Jenny knew the comment was aimed at her.

Alicia was looking at Steve all dewy-eyed, just like she had that time at the park when he'd called her *darlin'*. Jenny smiled at the memory of the picnic, the four of them, and the impromptu game of soccer, with Scott as the star. Then she nudged her daughter. "Eat your pie. The ice cream's melting."

When dessert was finished, the kids went back upstairs to their rooms. Steve helped Jenny clear the table and rinse the plates and cups to go in the dishwasher. "I should go," he said when they were finished. "And this time I really mean it."

Jenny smiled and wiped her hands on a towel. "I'll walk you out."

They stepped onto the porch where the night breeze sighed through a nearby pine. Steve hesitated, then leaned into her, touching her lips softly with his. The kiss was like a question, and Jenny answered by stepping closer and deepening the kiss. Quickly, the passion that had been dormant for so long roused from its slumber and burned low in her belly. Tongues touched and entwined, stirring heat in both of them, and Jenny could feel his hardness nudging urgently against her. Would he push her down on the hard wood of the porch and take her? Part of her was aghast at the thought, but another part of her wanted him to do just that.

He pulled back with a sharp intake of breath. "I'd forgotten how good you feel."

"I didn't forget," Jenny said when her breathing was under control. "I tried to, but ..." She let the rest drift off with a shrug.

"So nice to hear." Steve kissed her again, this time keeping it light and tantalizing. Then he broke the contact and said, "You can help me remember."

"When?"

"Are you free on Friday?"

She didn't even have to stop and think. She nodded. He smiled and walked away, leaving her to the evening music of tree frogs, crickets, and a night owl hooting somewhere in the distance.

THREE

AT SIX THE following Friday evening Jenny stood in her bedroom, trying to decide what to wear on her first date in what felt like forever. She had her cell phone tucked between shoulder and ear, talking to Carol, who was encouraging her to go with something really skimpy and sexy.

Jenny laughed. "I don't do skimpy and sexy well."

"Why not?"

"For one thing, I don't think I have a dress that qualifies. And even if I did, most restaurants keep the AC cranked so low, I'd freeze."

"Do you have time to go shopping?"

"No." Jenny moved the phone to her other ear and pushed clothes to one side in her closet. "Steve is picking me up in an hour. It'll take me that long to do something with my hair and maybe play with some makeup."

Carol chuckled, then said, "I should let you get to it. Call me later. I want all the details. Every last one of them."

"I'll call you if I am not otherwise occupied."

"Oooo. I like the sound of that."

23

When Jenny realized what her friend was thinking, Jenny laughed. "I meant sleeping."

"Yeah. Right." Carol laughed and ended the call.

An hour later, Jenny was dressed in a new pair of wide-legged gray slacks in a wool blend, a dark purple silk shirt, and a long cream-colored scarf that she draped twice around her neck. She'd clipped her hair back from her ears on each side to show off simple silver loop earrings. Nothing about the way she was dressed was particularly sexy, but it felt good. She smiled at her reflection in the long mirror on her closet door. Alicia had helped Jenny put the outfit together, and it turned out the girl had quite a knack for accessorizing.

A few minutes later, there was a knock on the door, and Jenny hurried to open it. Steve stood there, wearing pressed Levi's, a shirt almost the color of her scarf, and a dark brown suede jacket. Boots topped off the cowboy image. For a man who had grown up in the East, Steve did "cowboy" like a native Texan. Jenny smiled, and he did likewise.

"I'm leaving now," Jenny called toward the living room where Scott and Alicia were eating pizza while watching a taped episode of *Game of Thrones*. "You kids be good."

"You, too," Scott called out, a hint of laughter in his voice.

"That doesn't sound like much fun," Steve murmured as they stepped out and closed the door.

Steve did the gentlemanly thing, opening the passenger door to a bright red Kia Sportage. "New car?" Jenny asked, sliding into the smooth leather seat.

"Got it a few months ago."

Steve closed the door and went around to get in behind the wheel. Once he started the engine and pulled away from the curb, Jenny asked, "Where are we going?"

"Since I don't get many opportunities to drive this baby very far, I thought we'd run up to the WinStar Casino."

"I don't gamble."

"Neither do I. But they have a great restaurant and the ambiance is quite nice."

"Ambiance? Listen to you, all fancified."

"Well, darlin', a man can't be a hayseed his whole life."

That last was said with such a drawl; Jenny burst out laughing. Despite his way of dressing, Steve was anything but a hayseed. People often mistook small-town Texas cops for rubes, but many of those cops had come from big cities where they'd learned a thing or three about law enforcement. Jenny knew the real Steve Morrity from Baltimore.

Sighing, Jenny settled back into the comfortable seat, enjoying the ride and the silence. They'd learned two years ago that silence between them worked. Neither felt the need to jump in and fill any kind of void.

It took just under an hour to get to the casino just over the Texas border into Oklahoma. The jangle of bells and the screech of sirens as people won and lost at the slot machines greeted them as they walked into the large gaming room. The noise of all those machines and all the people talking and laughing and shouting made Jenny want to back out of the door. Steve seemed to sense her discomfort and, taking her arm, led her through the crowded floor to a hallway leading out of the cavernous room. "It's much quieter where we'll eat."

The noise slowly abated the further they went along the hall, and then Steve guided her toward an opening to The Grill restaurant. Soft music could be heard from hidden speakers, and a hostess seated them at a table covered with linen and set with fine china and crystal. "This is nice," Jenny said as they settled with menus.

"I've heard the steak is quite tasty," Steve said. "Linda told me about this place and recommended the filet."

Filet? Jenny couldn't remember the last time she'd had

anything but a chopped steak. Her mouth watered at the thought of a real steak, but the prices. *Oh my God.* She looked up at Steve. "Is that what you're having?"

"I think so. And how about the lobster bisque for an appetizer?"

Jenny bit her lip and leaned close to him to whisper. "I don't know what that is."

Steve burst out laughing and people at a nearby table looked over.

"Shhh," Jenny said. "People are staring."

Steve brought his laughter to a halt and whispered back. "It's a type of soup. You'll like it."

"How do you know about something that sounds so exotic?"

"Believe it or not, I have had some culture in my life. Katie was from Boston. We went back there a lot to visit her kinfolks. They had money."

"Oh." Jenny sat mute after that one word, not sure what else to say. The last time he'd talked about his deceased wife, it had been an awkward moment for them both. Tonight, there was no hint of the pain in his voice she'd remembered from when he'd told her about Katie and the cancer that had claimed her a few years before Jenny met him. But still. Jenny knew about grief and how the wrong word could trigger a sharp stab of pain.

Steve reached over and touched her hand. "It's okay. I can talk about her now without getting all soft and sappy."

Jenny smiled, relief washing over her, then glanced at the menu again. A young waitress with a hint of a tattoo peeking out from the cuff of her long-sleeved crisp white shirt stepped up. She wore black slacks, slung low on her hips, and a lovely smile graced her face. "You folks need some help with the menu?"

Jenny couldn't believe she was going to do this, but it was his dime. She looked at Steve, "Go ahead and order for us."

A look of surprise passed quickly over his face, as if he couldn't believe it either, then he turned to the waitress, ordering the lobster bisque for appetizers, with one order of calamari. Filets for both with a side of garlic mashed potatoes. He glanced over at Jenny. "Would you like a salad?"

She nodded, so he ordered the spinach salad.

"Would you like a wine, sir?"

Steve considered for just a moment then said, "A bottle of Cabernet Sauvignon."

Jenny put a hand to her mouth to cover a smile. He did know a lot more about fine dining than she did. When she ate out with her kids it was at Randy's Grill downtown, one or two steps above a McDonald's. Growing up on the wrong side of the tracks in a little town near San Antonio had not groomed her for high society.

Dinner was leisurely and enjoyable; the wine was tart and refreshing, and after a few glasses Jenny realized that neither one of them might be in shape to drive home. She declined a refill when Steve offered the last of the bottle to her, so he poured it into his glass. "Should we get some coffee?" she asked. "To, you know, be okay to drive?"

"We could do that if you want." He paused a moment then finished, "But we could just stay here until the wine buzz wears off."

Jenny glanced around the busy restaurant. "They might want this table."

"I didn't mean waiting here." The words were accompanied by a grin and a glint of mischief in his eyes. "Win-Star has a very nice hotel."

Jenny's eyes widened in surprise. "I couldn't. I mean ... I don't know."

Steve chuckled, then leaned over the table to rest his gaze on hers. "Two years ago, there was no doubt what was happening between us. And we both had to back away for a lot of reasons. I understand that. But now, there's nothing in our way. And I want you, Jenny. I really do."

Those last few words stole her heart. But still. Was he just hot to get her into bed and then nothing? "Was this part of your plan all along?"

He shook his head. "Not a definite plan. Just a thought. Or maybe a hope."

He settled back in his chair, apparently willing to give her all the time she needed to make up her mind. Desire warred with good sense. She'd never gone to bed with a man on a first date. Ever. But if she counted the dates with Steve from before, this wasn't the first date. Rationalizing to be sure, but she knew in her heart that there would be something after tonight.

The waitress walked up to the table. "Will there be dessert for you folks today?"

Jenny took a deep breath then asked, "Can we get it with room service?"

The waitress nodded. "Just call when you're ready." She left the bill on the table next to Steve.

When the young woman left, Steve looked at Jenny. "Are you sure?"

Jenny waited a long moment, then nodded.

After Steve paid the check, they went down the hall again, veering left to the entrance to the hotel. Steve walked to the desk to see if a room was available. One was. So he handed over his credit card.

"And how long will you be staying, sir?" The desk clerk asked, swiping the card and returning it.

"Just tonight."

The clerk seemed not to notice, or didn't care, that they had no luggage, and he handed over two keys. Jenny avoided meeting his eyes, lest her embarrassment show.

Once inside the room, all embarrassment melted away when Steve took her in his arms and kissed her. Soft and tentative at first, then with more assurance, their tongues touching then darting away. Holding the kiss, he slipped out of his jacket, and she reveled in the feel of firm muscles beneath the soft fabric of his shirt. It had been a long time. Too long.

Then his hands were on her breasts, lightly skimming her hardened nipples through the silk. Touching. Teasing. She thought her knees would buckle as the heat traveled down, awakening a feeling she'd almost forgotten.

Steve pulled back and looked at her. "I've wanted to do this for so long."

"Me, too," she murmured, taking off her scarf and letting it drift in a soft hush to the floor. "Me, too."

He slowly unbuttoned her shirt and trailed kisses across the top of her breasts. The touch of his lips sent fire through her body, and she reached down to brush her hand across the front of his pants. He moaned, then his breathing became harsh and swift.

The cadence of her breathing matched his, and she desperately wanted to feel skin on skin.

She took a half-step back and quickly undid the clasp of her slacks, kicking off her sandals as the fabric fell to her knees. Steve slowly pushed her shirt off her shoulders, then lowered the straps of her bra. She was now naked except for her panties.

Her new red silk panties.

Desire making her clumsy, Jenny fumbled with the clasp of his belt, then the metal button, then the zipper. Sliding the zipper down, her fingers brushed against him, and a gasp escaped his lips in a hot gust of breath against her face as he kissed her again. Her eyes. Her cheeks. Her chin. Then he captured her mouth again, pushing his tongue inside – long, slow, hard thrusts at first. Then their tongues found a mutual rhythm.

Jenny moaned, and Steve slid his mouth off of hers. He put his hands around her waist and guided her to the bed, the back of her knees just touching the edge.

"Lie down, Jenny," Steve said, his voice husky with passion. "I want to make love to you."

"I haven't done this in a long time."

"Me either. So let's make the most of this refresher course."

With one swift motion, she pulled the spread and blankets back and tossed them aside, then lowered herself to the fresh, crisp sheets. Then he was beside her, and the dance of their desire started again. Kisses burned her lips, and his hands celebrated her, stroking, loving, enticing.

Fire coursed through her, and she broke the kiss to murmur, "Oh, Steve. I need you inside me."

"Yes, ma'am."

"Are you prepared? You know, a condom?"

"Yes, ma'am. I was a Boy Scout. Always prepared."

"I always wanted to make love with a Boy Scout."

After just a moment of rustling tinfoil, Steve eased back down, slipping inside her with ease. Touching. Teasing. Touching again, then pulling away. Jenny wrapped her legs around his waist and pulled him in deep, cradling his head in her hands to match the thrusts of their bodies to the thrusts of their tongues.

Then Steve broke the kiss and slowed the movement, easing in and out of her in slow, agonizing thrusts. He rained kisses down her neck and onto her breasts, and again, she thought she would simply explode from wanting.

Then he pushed hard and deep, a new rhythm starting that moved them faster and faster, until a great shudder washed over Jenny from inside out. Steve continued the rhythm for a few more moments until they both stiffened in one great explosion of heat. He lay on top of her and whispered in her ear, "Oh Jenny darlin', that was perfect."

She sighed. Yes, it was.

Minutes later, Steve rolled over to one side, cradling Jenny into his chest, back to front. Neither spoke for the longest time, and Jenny was sure she could just close her eyes and go to sleep. Steve nuzzled the back of her neck. "We never did get dessert. Want me to call room service?"

Jenny chuckled. "No. I'm good."

As she said the words, she knew with all her being that she meant it. Being here with Steve. What they had just shared. It all felt so good. So natural. Like they truly did belong together.

Belonging.

Together.

As equals.

She'd never felt that way with Ralph. Not even in the beginning when the chemistry between them had sizzled. When it had come to sex. Especially the first time. Ralph had not made her feel as cherished, as loved, as celebrated as Steve had tonight. With Ralph, too often is was about satisfaction. Primarily his satisfaction.

"It's still early," Steve said. "We could stay a little while longer. Maybe we'll get hungry again."

Jenny didn't miss the inference in his voice that had nothing to do with strawberry shortcake or banana pudding. She smiled and snuggled closer to him, letting her eyelids fall. It was her answer. Not in words, but the message was clear.

Steve gave a sigh of contentment and held her.

She didn't know how long she'd slept, but the awakening was wonderful. Steve trailed kisses along her neck and across her shoulder. Then he paused and said, "Jenny? I'm getting a little hungry."

Coming fully awake, Jenny smiled and turned. "I think I am, too."

The second time around was just as incredible as the first had been, and afterward, while she lay panting on the sheets, Jenny wondered if they should stay and try for a trifecta. She remained still until their breathing returned to normal and the overhead fan cooled the sweat on their bodies. As tempting as the thought of staying was, Jenny knew that couldn't happen. It was late. Responsibilities tugged at her. "I'm going to take a quick shower," she said, slipping out of the bed and padding naked into the bathroom.

A few minutes later, the shower curtain slid back and Steve stepped in behind her. "Thought I'd conserve time and water," he said, slipping his hands around her waist.

Shower sex was pretty incredible, too, except for the struggle to maintain footing on the slick porcelain. And it turned out that they didn't save water or time.

Finally, pushing Steve gently away when he didn't seem ready to let go of her, Jenny said, "I'm getting out now. No more fooling around. I mean it."

There was laughter in her voice as she stepped out and grabbed a large, fluffy towel from the rack. Steve chuckled and turned off the water, then pushed the shower curtain aside. "Good thing, I'm thinking. Not sure this old man is up to any more fooling around."

Jenny turned and looked at him, his dark hair slick with water and still not showing much gray. A firm body that had just a hint of love handles at the waist. A light spattering of chest hair that was plastered against his skin. Also still dark. And the trail of hair that pointed the way down. Not much of what she could see looked old. "You're just fishing for a compliment."

"Oh, darlin'. You caught me out."

The grin that accompanied the statement almost made her change her mind about leaving, but she fought the temptation and walked out of the bathroom.

A few minutes later, they were both dressed, and Steve paused with his hand on the doorknob. "Last chance."

Jenny nudged his arm. "Open the door."

The drive home seemed to go faster than the drive to the casino, and Steve pulled in front of Jenny's house at just a little after one. He walked her to the door and waited until she got her key out, then he pulled her into a long, sweet kiss, before releasing her.

"It was a wonderful evening," Jenny said.

She could see the flash of his teeth in the moonlight as he smiled. "Oh, darlin'. Yes, it was."

He kissed her again, this time a feathery touch of lips on lips, then he said, "I'll call you."

Jenny knew those were not idle words. They were long past those teenage, or even young adult years, when it could be slam, bang, thank you, ma'am, no matter what was said. They both had waited so long for this, the statement had mountains of meaning. Tall mountains. She gave him one last quick kiss, then went inside. She hoped the kids were upstairs and not still up watching television. On Friday nights they could binge-watch Game of Thrones, no matter how many times they'd seen the episodes, and forget about time.

The living room was quiet and empty. Good. She was afraid that if they saw her, her grin might give something away. At least to Scott. Alicia may still be young enough to miss the tell-tale signs of a satisfied woman, but Jenny was sure Scott was astute enough to get it. She didn't pretend that he and Caitlin had never had sex. They'd been together as a couple since their freshman year in high school. Jenny had sat him down for "the talk" when the couple had first started dating. She knew how powerful teenage hormones could be. She could clearly remember her raging hormones back when Michael was conceived. So she had told Scott to be careful. Use protection. And please, don't do anything just to do it. Make it mean something. Sex is not just a game or an itch to be scratched. His face had turned the color of a radish when she said that, and he'd tried to brush her away, obviously not comfortable with the conversation, but she'd persisted until he'd given her an awkward nod of acknowledgement.

They hadn't talked about anything related to sex since. Truth be told, she hadn't been any more comfortable discussing it than he'd been listening to her. But it was one of those parental responsibilities she couldn't shirk.

Jenny hurried upstairs to her bedroom, slipped out of her clothes, and snuggled into bed. She didn't feel sleepy and was surprised when her eyelids became heavy and that first gray wave of slipping into the world of dreams washed over her.

Good sex was better than warm milk any day.

FOUR

SATURDAY MORNING SHAFTS of sunlight streaming through the open curtains and spilling onto her bed woke Jenny. She'd forgotten to close the curtains last night. Oh, well. She stretched, and a smile played across her lips as she thought of the night before. She would have stayed in bed, savoring those thoughts longer, but she had to get up to go to work. Normally Saturdays were short workdays, but not this one. It was homecoming weekend, and she had a bunch of mums to finish by that evening.

She jumped out of bed, took a quick shower, and was dressed and out the door in less than fifteen minutes. The kids were still in bed, and she knew they would be at home the rest of the day, with Scott getting ready for the dance that evening and Alicia wanting to help him with every detail.

Enough time had passed since the break-in that some of Jenny's anxiety had begun to wane. It helped that the daily routine of the shop was back to normal, with Jenny and Mitchell running full speed to keep up with orders.

Finding the front door unlocked brought a flare of alarm,

but this time when she called out for Mitchell, she got an answer. She went in to find him standing in the doorway leading to the back. "Thought I'd get a head start on the mums," he said as she came in and closed the door.

"Great." Jenny followed him to the design area, making a quick stop to drop her purse and sweater in the office. She joined Mitchell, nodding approval when she saw that he had ribbons cut and flowers out.

They had been working for a couple of hours, setting aside the finished mums to work on the next, when Jenny paused for a moment, fingering a piece of pale-yellow ribbon and smiling. This mum was for Scott and Caitlin, and her heart warmed as she thought about the young couple and how special this night would be. Then her mind made the leap to last night, and her smile broadened as she thought about dinner with Steve. Actually, thinking about more than just the dinner.

She didn't know that Mitchell had noticed her smile until he said, "You are looking incredibly in bliss. Harried is the look you usually have on Homecoming Day."

"In bliss?"

"Yes. A certain expression that says, 'I'm so incredibly happy.'"

Jenny had to laugh and was glad for the moment of distraction. She didn't want to tell her partner exactly what she'd been thinking about that put her in bliss. He didn't need to know about the crazy, wonderful sex, but she did like his phrase 'in bliss.' And he could know about Steve. "I had a date with Steve last night."

Mitchell stopped focusing on the bow he was making with another piece of yellow ribbon and looked at her full on. "Oh, do tell."

"We had a very tender steak, and some lobster soup, and ..." Oh, they'd totally forgotten to order dessert.

"And?"

She mentally scrambled for an answer. "A bottle of red wine."

"Something in there must have been very tasty for you to be grinning like that."

The warmth of a blush touched her cheeks, and Jenny giggled. My God, she hadn't giggled since she was fifteen. "Yes. Yes, it was. But enough about that. We need to get back to work."

"This man can talk while he works," Mitchell said, turning back to the mum he was arranging. "So tell me. Will you be seeing Steve again?"

"Yes. I've added him to my 'to do' list."

When Mitchell burst out laughing, Jenny realized the implication. "Oh, my God! That isn't what I meant. Please stop laughing."

"Oh dear." Mitchell wiped tears off his cheeks. "This is so refreshing. You are such a dear."

Jenny knew why Mitchell had a hard time abandoning himself to laughter. The wild carnival ride he'd been on with Jeffery's health after the HIV diagnosis sometimes had Mitchell wound tighter than a banjo string. But she knew he didn't want to talk about it unless he broached the subject first, and she understood that need. So she simply smiled and said, "I'm so glad I could amuse you."

Mitchell continued to chuckle as he made the finishing touches to the mum, then set it aside to start another.

By the end of the day, thirty mums had made it out the door, the last of the orders they had worked on for most of the week. Using soft tissue paper, Jenny carefully wrapped the mum she'd made for Scott and took it home.

It was six o'clock when she pulled into the driveway beside her house and got out of the car, carefully retrieving the mum and the matching garter from the back seat of her Ford Escape. She walked into the house and saw Scott and Caitlin waiting near the front entry. He looked very sharp, and very grown-up, in the vintage suit he'd found in the second-hand shop in town. It hadn't needed any alteration, and the charcoal coat with wide lapels fit his broad shoulders perfectly. His coral-colored shirt had a few ruffles in front and lace trim on the cuffs that peeked out from his sleeves. He and Caitlin had decided to go retro, hence the suit and shirt. She was wearing a white lace dress with a high neck and pearl buttons down the front of the bodice. Jenny looked from one to the other, realizing they could be decked out for a wedding, not a high school dance. She also realized that she wouldn't mind at all if they were to marry. Just not for a few years.

Jenny walked over and hugged Caitlin. "You look lovely."

"Thanks."

Alicia ran in from the kitchen, carrying an apple with several bites gone. "About time you got here. I was afraid they'd leave without the flowers."

"We wouldn't do that," Scott said, giving his sister a playful nudge.

Jenny chuckled and hugged her son before unwrapping the mum and handing it to him. "I'm not sure where you can pin it on her dress."

They all looked at the delicate lace of Caitlin's dress, then Alicia said, "Why don't you just carry it?"

"Good idea," Caitlin said.

Since they had asked for a smaller version of the traditional mums that often had ribbons hanging down for several feet and lots of ornamentation, carrying was possible. This small arrangement had purple and yellow carnations, the school colors, sprigs of baby's breath, and three pale yellow ribbons in varying lengths, the longest only about twelve inches. To personalize the arrangement, Scott had asked that Jenny include a picture of him with Michael when they were young. The photo showed two little boys splashing in the backyard pool and grinning – Michael with a full set of perfect white teeth, Scott missing the two in front. When Scott handed her the picture he'd kept on his dresser, Jenny didn't comment on his choice. She merely gave him a slight nod and swallowed the lump in her throat.

For the garter decoration, Caitlin had given a picture of herself as a baby, all pudgy, pink cheeks and a toothless grin that lit up her face.

The choices were sweet and memorable, and Jenny was sure the young couple would make tonight so special they would carry those memories for a long time. She took a few pictures with her phone to share later with her mom and her brother – and Ralph. Sharing with Ralph was still very much an afterthought, but at least she thought of him now. There were too many years when thoughts didn't pass back and forth at all, but he was trying to make an effort, so she could, too.

Jenny hugged them both, whispering to Scott, "I love you. Be safe," and then watched from the porch as they went to Scott's old Honda Civic. He'd bought the car with money earned making deliveries for Jenny and working part-time at the local hardware store. Yesterday, he'd cleaned the bright red car inside and out, and the exterior gleamed in the fading daylight. Jenny was pleased to see he did the gentlemanly thing and opened the passenger door for Caitlin before walking around to slide into the driver's seat and pull away from the curb.

Watching the car grow smaller in the distance, a mix of emotions overwhelmed Jenny. Love for Scott and the woman who seemed destined to be his life-mate. Excitement for them as they embarked on a special night. That niggle of apprehension whenever he got in his car and drove away, hoping that he would make it back. Her final words to him were always the same, "I love you. Be safe." And she knew those words meant more to Scott than they would have before the accident that took Michael out of their lives. Some things meant more to all of them since the accident.

Chasing the thoughts aside, Jenny went back into the house. It was pizza night for her and Alicia.

Maybe a good animated movie would take her mind off of Steve and that glorious night and the little worry that she couldn't shake. Did it mean as much to him? Did she dare hope for the future?

So, okay. More than one little worry.

FIVE

ON MONDAY, Steve was in the break room at the station, getting some of the sludge that was sometimes called coffee, when Chief Gonzales walked in. Gonzales always looked more like a Spanish aristocrat than a small-town cop. Part of the image came from his tall, thin stature and the way he held his head high, his chin pointed up just a bit. The rest came from the nicely tailored suits he wore, jacket buttoned except when he was seated. "Got a minute?" he asked Steve.

"Sure. Got something for me on the burglaries?"

Gonzales shook his head. "My office."

That last was said with a sharp tone of authority that Gonzales rarely used. He preferred the same team approach that Steve did and seldom pulled rank. This was an exception, and a wave of apprehension washed over Steve. What the hell could be wrong? It wouldn't do to try to guess, if even just mentally, so Steve carried the cup of coffee with him as he followed the chief down the hall.

Gonzales took a seat behind his desk, motioning to Steve to sit across from him in the small chair with a leather seat. Steve complied, wondering about the solemn expression on the other man's face. "Something wrong?"

"Got a call from the mayor this morning."

While it was not the possible bad news Steve was anticipating, like a death in the Gonzales family, it wasn't good news. The Chief answered directly to the mayor, who was a thumb-in-every-pie kind of guy. The mayor seldom called to pat the Chief on the back.

"What's the current bug up his ass?"

"You."

Steve choked on his coffee, splatters of brown dotting the front of his white shirt. He dabbed at them with a tissue from the box on the desk.

"What for?"

"Stepping over professional boundaries."

"What?"

"Dating a crime victim."

"Wait." Steve took a moment to let the words sink in. "You mean Jenny Jasik? Who says we're dating?"

"You're not the only one who goes to the casino," Gonzales said. "Unfortunately, you picked the same night our esteemed mayor was there with his wife."

Steve shook his head in dismay. "I didn't see them."

"Mark said you were hurrying out of the restaurant. Looked like you had somewhere important to be."

Heat crawled up Steve's cheeks. Just like some teenage kid caught buying a condom at the drugstore. Back when that action made kids blush.

Of course, Gonzales noticed. He was a trained investigator. Gonzales chuckled, then said, "I won't ask."

"Thank you."

"But I will have to tell you to stop seeing her. It's against policy."

"Wait a minute. That was when we worked together. This is different."

"No. Officers cannot associate with victims of crimes." Gonzales leaned back in his chair. "Do you need a refresher on that part of the law enforcement code book?"

"No. I remember. Just figured nobody would have to know."

"Oh, come on." Gonzales came forward so quickly, Steve thought the man might fly right across the desk. "The mayor already knows. He'll nail both our asses to the wall if people start talking. And they will."

"So? What? I have to pass up the first chance I've had for love since ..."

The rest of the words couldn't come, but Steve knew Gonzales could finish for him. The Chief had been right beside him for weeks after Katie had died. He knew how long it had taken Steve to even be able to smile, let alone consider a serious relationship.

"I'm sorry," Gonzales said, his voice softening. "On a personal level, I wouldn't do this. But I have no choice. Cops are under a magnifying glass now. You know that. A few less than stellar guys making it bad for all of us. And this is an election year for our esteemed mayor."

"Screw him."

Gonzales made a show of covering his ears for a moment then dropping his hands. "Did you say something? I must have missed it."

Steve chuckled, but then the smile disappeared. "I don't want to lose Jenny."

Gonzales didn't answer for a long moment, and then he said, "Then find that burglar."

Steve went back to his office and threw the remains of his coffee, and the Styrofoam cup, in the trash, before slumping in his chair. Jeez! What a royal fuck up. And after last Friday night. It had been everything he'd hoped for and more, so what was he going to do now? More importantly, how could he tell Jenny? There was no way he could NOT tell her, but, man, it wasn't a prospect he looked forward to.

He swung back and forth in his chair, considering his options, which didn't include telling her in a phone call. That would really be a coward's way out. Then he remembered a bit of advice his mother had given him when he had to apologize to a classmate for hitting him with a basketball in PE, "Don't put off what you've got to do. Just get it over with."

So, okay. He'd go talk to Jenny. He glanced at his watch. Almost four. He could go by the shop now. Get it over with. And if any of the mayor's spies saw him, he could always say it was official police business. It wouldn't do to say, "Screw you," although that's what he'd like to say to those people who reported on the cops.

———

After hearing the tell-tale creak of the floor in the front, Jenny walked out of the design area, drying her hands on a towel looped over her belt. Expecting a customer, she was delighted to see Steve standing there, but her delight started to fade when she noticed his grim expression and the way he twirled his hat around and around in his hands. "What's wrong?"

"Is Mitchell here?"

The question caught her off guard. "What?" Alarm raced through her. "He left early. Did something happen to him or Jeffery?"

"No." Steve stepped forward and laid a hand on her arm. "I am so sorry to have scared you. Can we go in the back and talk?"

The somber tone of his voice continued to raise all kinds of alarms for Jenny. "I am not budging until you assure me that nothing awful has happened."

"Nobody you know has been hurt. At least not physically," Steve said. "But there is something we need to talk about. In private."

Jenny thought about all the possible subjects they needed to talk about in private, and the only one she liked would not have put that serious expression on Steve's face. She sighed. "We can go to my office."

Once settled in the small space adjoining the design area, both of them on metal folding chairs on either side of the small oak desk used for the paperwork involved with the business, Jenny shot Steve an unmistakable look. "Okay. Talk."

Again, Steve twisted his hat. "I've been ordered to stop seeing you."

"What? It's a joke, right? A piss-poor joke, but a joke, right?"

Steve shook his head, mangling his hat even more. Jenny reached out and grabbed it away. "Don't kill your poor Stetson."

"You're worried about my hat?"

"Yes. No. Maybe I'll just stomp on it for you while you tell me the rest."

So he did. About the mayor. The phone call. The edict from Gonzales. The failed attempt to try to find a way around the policy. Jenny tried to let the words settle. Let them make sense. But they didn't. They rattled around in the space between them like kernels of dried corn, and every now and then a few of them popped. Like the final ones. "So, we can't go out or be seen together."

Jenny thought for a moment, then asked, "Until when?"

"We catch the person breaking into the businesses downtown."

"Okay. I'll help."

Steve shook his head.

"Why not?"

"You can't, Jenny. Helping us before was a one-time thing. There's no way Gonzales will let you get involved in this."

Tears burned in Jenny's eyes, and she blinked to hold them back. She didn't want to cry. Okay. Maybe she did. But she also wanted to scream. And she really did want to stomp on the hat. Anything to vent the frustration and anger that was building up inside her like the core of a volcano. Any minute she would erupt. She turned away from him and pounded on her thigh.

After a moment, she felt movement behind her, then Steve took her hands and stilled them. After another moment, he pulled her to her feet, turning her to face him again. "Before I go, and while we are hidden back here where nobody can see us ..." His lips stopped forming words and touched hers in a gentle, comforting kiss. A kiss that he quickly turned from gentle to passionate.

Jenny's body responded in kind, and she seriously thought about going to lock the front door.

Steve pulled back, taking both her shoulders in his hands and holding her gaze with his. "That was a promise, Jenny. The kiss. I will catch that burglar, and I will be back."

Despite the seriousness of the moment, an urge to laugh almost overtook her. The line from *The Terminator* flashed through her mind. She knew the wild mix of emotions was making her think of that. Her mind always did crazy things to compensate for pain.

"What?" Steve asked.

At first, she wasn't sure what he meant, then she realized.

Of course. He'd picked up on the subtle change in her mood. "I thought about calling you Arnold."

"Arnold?"

She quoted the famous line, complete with accent, and Steve chuckled. "When I come back, maybe I'll be naked, too."

"That would be fine by me."

Then she didn't want to smile anymore. She leaned into him, resting her head on his chest where she heard the thump, thump, thump of his heart. He combed his fingers through her hair in a slow, rhythmic caress. "I'll do my best to get this guy quickly."

"Can you let me know how the investigation progresses?"

"Of course. As one of the victims, you are entitled to updates."

"Victim." Jenny shuddered. "How I hate that word. Makes me feel so weak."

Steve pulled back and smiled at her. "You, darlin', are anything but weak."

The darlin' unraveled her again, and tears spilled out of her eyes in a hot torrent. Steve brushed them off her cheeks with his thumbs, then kissed her again before heading to the door.

Jenny let him go out alone. It was an abrupt departure, but the kind they both needed. She knew this was as hard for Steve as it was for her. To have finally gotten together only to be pulled apart again. Knowing how long it took for some cases to be resolved, Jenny did not hold out much hope that he would be back next week to pick up where they left off today. "Damn, damn, double damn."

She would have said much worse, but she'd been trying not to drop the f-bomb as much as she used to. Even the language that had been associated with that awful time around Michael's death grated on her nerves and felt awkward on her tongue.

Jenny dried the rest of her tears and cleaned up where

she'd been working, putting away ribbons and wiping scraps of paper and pieces of flower stems from the design table. Then she closed up the shop and went out to her car, where she just sat for a few minutes. A great sadness hung heavy on her shoulders, and there was no way she could go home and pretend everything was okay. She called Scott on his cell and asked if he would stay home with Alicia this evening. Not that Alicia needed a sitter, but Jenny hated to leave either of the kids alone. Scott agreed that he could fix something for dinner and have it ready when Alicia came home from cheer practice. "You okay, Mom?" he asked before she could hang up. "You sound a little funny."

"I'm fine." She tried to smile, hoping that could transfer to her voice.

"You don't sound fine."

"Low battery on my phone. Gotta run." She hung up before he could ask another question. Unlike many teenage boys who only half-listened to a parent, especially a mother, Scott was attuned to her in a way that not even Michael had been. At times Jenny loved that, but there were times like this that she halfway wished he'd be more interested in a video game on his phone and not the note of anxiety in his mother's voice.

Before starting the car, Jenny dialed another number.

Carol.

At a time like this, a girl needed a friend and a tall glass of wine. Hell, maybe a whole bottle of wine.

SIX

"DO YOU WANT TO MEET SOMEWHERE?" Carol asked.

"No," Jenny said. "Polish your wine glasses. I'm on my way."

About forty minutes later, Jenny was at Carol's, after a stop at the liquor store for a bottle of Chardonnay and another of White Zinfandel. She'd brushed away Carol's questions at the door, and now they were in the living room, seated at opposite ends of Carol's large white sectional. "You sure you want us drinking wine on your new sofa?" Jenny asked.

"I'm so glad you brought white," Carol said, offering a hint of a smile.

They sipped in silence for a few minutes, then Carol said, "I've waited long enough. What put that pained expression on your face?"

The volcano erupted, mostly in tears that seared Jenny's cheeks like hot lava.

Carol jumped up, sloshing a bit of her wine on the floor,

and rushed to her friend. "What happened? Tell me. Are the kids okay? Your mother?"

"Whoa," Jenny said, snuffling back the tears. "Didn't mean to scare you. They're fine." She took a deep breath and continued. "Steve and I ... we can't see each other."

"He broke up with you? After one date?"

Jenny held up a finger, digging in her purse that was beside her on the sofa. After pulling out a tissue, she wiped her face and then told her friend the whole awful story.

"Shit. That sucks."

"Tell me about it." Jenny tried for a smile, but it faltered.

"Come here, girlfriend." Carol pulled Jenny close for a good, long hug.

After a few moments, Carol released her and went to refill their wine glasses. "Now I know why you brought two bottles."

Once Carol was once again settled on the sofa, she said, "Too bad you can't go back and un-report the break-in."

Jenny gave a feeble laugh. "I would if I could. I'd also like to catch the bastard who did that."

"Oh, God, no! Don't even tell me if you're thinking what I think you're thinking."

This time Jenny did laugh, and some of the tension in her neck eased. "Steve was clear. I am not to do anything."

"Good man. And you're going to do what he says. Right?"

Jenny thought about that for a moment. She never did like to be told what to do. She'd been called a stubborn, willful child by her mother most of her life. The last time not too long ago. So a direct order always triggered a contrary response.

On the other hand, she knew that Steve could face serious consequences should she try to investigate and get into any kind of trouble. He had made that so very clear when she was working as a CI on the drug case, and when that had been over, she'd sworn to let that be her last foray into the dark world of police work.

Still, that had been then, and it is always easy to make definitive decisions while not knowing what could happen in the future.

Jenny took a hefty swallow of her wine, then set the glass down on the burnished oak coffee table. "I know I should. Do what Steve said, I mean, but the truth is I cannot just step aside."

Carol shook her head. "Despite what happened last time you played Wonder Woman?"

Jenny didn't respond. She didn't know what to say. One part of her brain – probably the logic side – said to just let it go. Let the professionals do their job. But another part of her brain – probably the part that released all those endorphins of satisfaction – said to step up. Take action. Don't sit back like a victim.

Carol twirled the wine in her glass, then looked intently at Jenny. "You're going to do it, aren't you."

It wasn't a question.

Jenny sighed. "Until two minutes ago, I was going to do what Steve said."

"You still can, you know."

"I could."

"But you won't."

Jenny nodded. "Steve told me that, most likely, these robberies are being done by users. Needing money to buy more drugs. I happen to know a few of those folks."

"No. No. No." Carol shook her head emphatically. "You can't get involved with that whole drug scene again. Remember last time?"

"How could I forget?"

Silence reigned for a few moments, and Jenny knew that

Carol was remembering last time, too, and how it had torn their lives apart. Thankfully, they both had healed since then. Well, healed as much as they could be considering what they both had lost. Carol the man she'd thought was her forever man. And Jenny? Jenny had lost a part of herself when she'd pulled the trigger and sent a bullet to bring death to a man. One moment alive and breathing. The next dead, a body slumped against a wall splattered with his blood.

Carol sighed. "I can't change your mind, can I."

Again, not a question, but Jenny shook her head anyway.

"What about Steve?"

"This time I won't be doing this officially. He doesn't have to know."

"Do you think that's wise?"

"Probably not. But you know what? Taking action like I did two years ago. That felt good. Damn good. And I was willing to sacrifice that feeling of satisfaction to be able to have Steve in my life. But now? Now everything has changed. And now I'm willing to do anything I have to to blast through that barrier that was erected between us."

"I don't have any dynamite, and I got rid of my guns."

The first part of the comment was a joke and Jenny chuckled, but she recognized the seriousness underneath the second part. She remembered. Carol had once been an avid sharp-shooter competitor, but that interest in weapons had ended when the gun she'd loaned Jenny had taken a life to save another.

Killing paper targets was one thing, but people?

Never.

Jenny nodded. "No guns. I'm just going to ask around and try to get a name. Somebody who knows somebody who's bankrolling his habit at the expense of the businesses in town. Then maybe persuade that somebody to go to the police."

"Ha! You make it sound so simple. It's not that simple, girlfriend."

————

After sobering up with two cups of coffee at Carol's, Jenny drove home around midnight and went in through the back door, easing out of her shoes when the door was locked behind her. Tiptoeing in her stocking feet, she stepped on the inside edges of the stairs, not wanting to hit a board that creaked in the middle and wake the kids this late on a school night.

She might as well have walked into the house and brought a full orchestra with her. The minute she reached the top landing, Scott came out of his room, not looking the least bit sleepy. "Where have you been? I was worried sick."

He'd kept his voice low, but the inherent challenge still rankled.

"Remember who's the parent here," she whispered back.

He leaned closer. "Remember who made us sign the pact that we'd always check in with each other?"

Jenny took a breath and let it out slowly. Scott took a step back and said, "You smell like a brewery."

"I told you I was going to visit Carol. We had some wine." Jenny brushed past him and headed toward her room. "And now I'm going to bed."

Scott followed her to the door, still keeping his voice low. "Something's wrong. I can tell."

Jenny sighed. Scott was not going to let this go. In the two years since Michael's death, and what followed afterward, they'd all developed a heightened awareness of mood and tone of voice. They lived with an inner anxiety that didn't seem to want to go away no matter how hard they tried to act normal. Pretend everything was normal.

Yes. Some things were normal. The rising and setting of the sun. The daily routines that gave them something to focus on. The few hours each day when thoughts of Michael would not intrude. But the lasting legacy of losing someone you loved was this super sensitivity. If Jenny did not reassure Scott, he would stay awake for hours longer, worrying. Flitting from one awful possibility to another like a hummingbird that couldn't settle.

She turned. "Okay. This is going to be the short version of what is going on. We both need to get to bed. Steve dropped a bombshell on me today. He was told that we cannot date until the burglary at the shop is solved."

"That's stupid. Why?"

"Policy."

Scott was silent for a moment, then he asked, "Are you okay?"

Jenny stifled the impulse to laugh. That was always such a lame question, but one that was asked in so many situations: fires, accidents, other tragedies. Newscasts were filled with grieving people having a microphone shoved in their face and being hit with that stupid question. If they were okay, would they be staring up at their burning house with tears flowing down their cheeks? Geesh!

Jenny took in another deep breath and let it out slowly. "No. I am not okay. That's why I went to Carol's and drank wine and cried and cussed."

That elicited a chuckle from Scott, and Jenny reached up to plant a kiss on his cheek before giving him a little push in the chest. "Now go to bed. Any more questions about this have to wait until tomorrow."

SEVEN

IT WAS a few days before Jenny could manage to get out in the evening to see if she could make any connections to the drug users who'd bought from her before. Since her role in the takedown of that main supplier had been hush-hush, she was sure word had not gotten to the street about who had a part in the drama that had ended with a change of leadership in the drug business. Pretty sure, that is.

This time she was determined not to let her secret sleuthing interfere with family responsibilities. Tuesday night, she cheered Scott on to victory in a soccer game. Since this was his last year to play, she'd been trying to be diligent about going to the games. Wednesday, Alicia needed a ride to Youth Group at the church that she'd joined shortly after Michael died. Belonging to that church had become very important to her, and it didn't seem to bother her that she was the only one in the family to attend services. Jenny had thought about asking Scott to do chauffeur duty that night, but changed her mind. She'd asked him too many times already.

So, today, Thursday, she was putting on the skimpy top and

tight black jeans she'd worn when she was "Connie just looking for a little fun" two years ago. Geesh! What had ever possessed her to pick a name like that? No wonder it had taken so long for her to be accepted into the local drug scene.

She hadn't told the kids in advance what she was going to do. Didn't want to deal with all their questions about it. So tonight, she just walked into the living room and stood for a moment until they looked up from the TV. Scott paused the program and looked at her. "What're you doing dressed like that?"

"Going out."

He shook his head, apparently making the connection to the past. "Really? Is this like an instant replay of before? You said you were done with all that."

"I am. Was. Now I'm just trying to help Steve catch the burglars."

The kids looked at her, mute for a moment, and then Alicia asked, "How are you going to do that?"

"See if someone will give me a name or two as possibilities."

"Oh, like that will really happen," Scott said. "Get real. Nobody wants to be a snitch."

"I didn't say it was going to work." Jenny took in a long breath, then let it out slowly. "But I just want to try. Okay? I can't sit around and do nothing."

Another moment of silence that Alicia finally broke. "I like it better when you're just a normal mom. This is too scary."

"I'm not doing anything scary this time. Honest. Just talking to some of the people on the street."

Scott snorted. "Haven't you heard? The street is a dangerous place. Isn't that what you keep warning us about?"

"The streets aren't as bad as they once were," Jenny said. "Since we took down that supplier outside of town, the drug trade has slowed to a trickle around here."

"Well, that trickle is still apparent. We see some of those druggies hanging out at the Sonic in town. And they don't look friendly."

Jenny appreciated his concern. And at least this time he was being more mature about how he expressed it, but still. This was her decision. She looked at both of the kids in turn then said, "Trust me. What I am going to be doing for a few nights is not nearly as dangerous as what I did before. And I will be very, very careful."

Alicia ran over and gave her a hug. "I wish you didn't have to do it."

"I know, honey."

Scott didn't say anything, or make a move toward her. He pointed the remote at the TV and started the program again.

Well, that was that.

———

Steve let the patrol car roll slowly down Main Street. It was the first time he'd been on night patrol in a long time, but Henson had called in sick and someone had to cover the shift. Steve figured he might as well rack up some overtime and have something to keep himself occupied so he wouldn't think about Jenny. Not that the plan was working so well. He'd already made two passes in front of her shop, so he could hardly keep her out of his consciousness.

Wouldn't it be a great stroke of luck to catch the burglar and end this mess they were in?

Steve chuckled at the thought, but also kept a watchful eye on the stores as he first passed in front, and then turned to check the alleys behind both sides of Main Street. Most of the burglaries had been in a five-block section of Main that housed Jenny's floral shop, a few antique stores, a fabric store, a small art gallery, a framing and arts supply store, a candy store, a few clothing stores for men and women, and a couple of small restaurants. So far, the burglaries had been clustered in the first three blocks, and Steve was focusing on the other two tonight.

After his third pass behind the stores with no sign of criminal activity, Steve decided to take a break and roll by the Dairy Queen for a soda. Instead of the drive-through, he elected to park and go inside. He needed to stretch his legs. He got out, locked the car and headed across the lot.

That's when he saw her.

Jenny?

No, it couldn't be. The woman was talking to a kid at one of the tables in the courtyard area. The kid, a young teen, kept looking around furtively, and when he spotted Steve coming toward them, he jumped up and ran. That's when the woman turned and faced him full on.

It was Jenny.

He started to walk toward her, but she gave him a frantic look, then shook her head ever so slightly before standing quickly and hurrying away.

Steve went inside and got a cola before going to sit at the same table where Jenny had been talking to the kid. After waiting a few minutes, he pulled out his cell phone and dialed her number.

She answered, her voice a bit wary.

"What the hell, Jenny!? Was that a drug dealer you were talking to?"

"Can I answer one question at a time?"

Steve blew out a breath in exasperation. "All right. What are you doing?"

"Trying to help."

Steve blew out another breath, glad he was not with her at the moment. He wanted to shake her until her teeth rattled.

"Even though you were told to stay out of it, you decided to 'help' anyway?"

If Jenny picked up on the sarcasm, she didn't react in a typical manner. Something that Steve had always found endearing about her. She wasn't typical.

"I told you I couldn't just sit back and—"

"And I told you that's exactly what you should do."

Despite the fact that his voice was rising, hers became quite still. "Do you at least want to hear what I found out?"

That stumped him for a moment. Then he said, "Sure."

"That kid was pretty chatty. You would have thought we were pals or something. I scored some weed from him."

"I can't hear that."

"Then we were best buds. I started talking about the burglaries on Main. Told him the cops had even talked to me."

"He believed you?"

"Yeah. The truth is always convincing."

Steve chuckled.

"I asked if he'd been questioned and he said no. Seemed to be impressed that I was a bad girl. Bad enough to be a suspect. Anyway, he mentioned this girl he knows. Yolanda. She was griping about her boyfriend making her do things she didn't want to do."

"Did he say what? Or give a last name?"

"Answering your questions in order. No and no."

"That's not much."

"No. But it's something. Right? You can look for this girl Yolanda?"

"Yeah." Steve rubbed a hand across his cheek. "We'll check the databases and see what we come up with."

Jenny didn't respond for a moment, and Steve said, "You still there?"

"Yes."

"Thought I'd lost you."

"No. Just a bit of a letdown."

"Wanted to solve the case all by yourself?"

That elicited a chuckle. "Of course not. That's what the police are for."

"I'm glad you see my point, finally."

Jenny laughed again, and Steve had to smile. They had come full circle, but ended on a much better note than where they had started. He wished he didn't have to hang up, but four more hours of patrol loomed ahead of him before Linda would take over. "Gotta, run, Jenny. This was a lot of help. Really. So you can stop playing detective."

"I wasn't playing."

Her tone held a bit of ice, and Steve wondered what had happened to the banter and the laughter. He'd meant that last sentence as a joke. Didn't she get that? Then he realized maybe not. They were both on an emotional roller coaster again. "I know, Jen," he said. "Didn't mean to insult you."

Steve heard a deep sigh from the other end, and then Jenny said, "It's okay. Well, actually not really. This whole mess sucks. But we're okay."

Now Steve could hang up with a smile, hoping the *okay* would last until they caught the asshole who was ruining a perfectly good relationship.

EIGHT

JENNY SAT on the porch with Alicia, passing out Halloween candy. It was one of Jenny's favorite nights of the year, and she loved decorating the yard with pumpkins, ghosts, and skeletons. She didn't do spiders. She hated spiders, even the pretend ones, although Alicia had snuck some webbing and a big black tarantula in the low branches of the tree. That was okay. It was far enough away that Jenny could ignore it.

The breeze picked up, and Jenny pulled the long black cape around her shoulders against the chill in the air. The wide brim of the pointy black hat fell over her forehead, and she brushed it back when a girl about five years old, dressed as Dora the Explorer, came up. "Trick or treat," the girl said.

"Certainly Dora wouldn't do any nasty tricks," Jenny said, pulling a handful of candy out of the large ceramic pumpkin next to her on the porch, but not putting it in the bag.

The girl gave her a puzzled look and Jenny had to smile. So many of the kids, especially the young ones, were so surprised when she talked to them instead of just dropping candy into opened bags.

"You'll have to forgive my mom," Alicia said, poking her mother with her elbow and nodding to the girl's bag. "She thinks you should earn your candy."

"By a trick?" A little frown of puzzlement creased the girl's forehead. "My brother said you only trick if people don't give you candy."

"Have you tricked anyone yet?" Alicia asked.

The girl shook her head. "I don't even know what trick to do."

"Tell you what," Jenny said. "Why not make it a smile and a very loud 'thank you'? Then I'll give you the candy."

A smile brightened the girl's face and she shouted, "Thank you."

"You're welcome." Jenny dropped the candy in the sack and the girl scampered to the next house.

Alicia stood and walked into the house, coming back out in a few minutes with her *Harry Potter* Gryffindor scarf around her neck.

"Going trick or treating?" Jenny asked.

"No." Alicia sat down in the chair on the other side of the pumpkin. "I was just cold."

"If you borrow my black robe, you could almost have a costume."

Alicia laughed. "That's okay." She grabbed a bite-sized Mounds bar out of the candy stash. "Why do you still dress up every Halloween anyway?"

There had been a lull in the parade of kids for the past five minutes, so Jenny grabbed a candy bar for herself and opened it before answering. "Believe it or not, your father and I really liked Halloween when we were dating and first married."

"Really?"

Jenny nodded and then took a bite of the Baby Ruth, chewing a while before continuing. "It's always been a favorite of mine. Holiday, that is. I hated it when Grandma said I was too old to go begging for candy. Not that I wanted the candy so much. Although that was part of it. But I just liked the idea of dressing up and pretending to be someone else. And I liked the ghosts and goblins and all the rest of the Halloween hype."

"But not the spiders," Alicia said, gesturing to her creation in the tree.

Jenny laughed. "Not the spiders."

"It is fun," Alicia said, looking down the street where a new group of kids was approaching. Even from a distance they could both hear the loud chatter and laughter. Alicia turned to her mother. "When did it stop being fun for Daddy?"

That question took Jenny by surprise. Alicia didn't ask about her father that much. She just seemed happy to be able to see him, and hadn't shown a great deal of curiosity about past history.

Jenny finished the candy bar and crumpled the wrapper as she thought about her answer. The last vestiges of fun had gone out of their marriage shortly after Scott had been born. It was as if being responsible for one more person had tipped Ralph over some edge. Edge of what, Jenny had never been sure. He had just started working longer hours. Staying away even when he wasn't working. And being irritable and short-tempered when he was home. She had started to be glad when he was away.

Until the bimbo had appeared on the scene.

But that was not something she wanted to tell her thirteen-year-old daughter who loved her father.

"When your father started to work lots more hours, he didn't have time for playing or for fun," Jenny said. "I don't think he decided that. It just happened."

That was a lie, but the truth would pierce her daughter. Ralph had made some pretty awful choices in the last few years they had been married. Luckily for all of them, he was making better choices now.

"Do you still love him?"

Wow. Another question out of left field. Maybe it was the dark. The quiet as that group of kids veered off and went around the corner. The pleasant evening that invited this kind of conversation. As Jenny formulated an answer, she knew this time it had to be the truth, and she should be direct. "No. I don't love him. Not like I did once. But I do care. We share so much." Jenny reached across to pat Alicia on the knee. "You can't have kids together and not care."

"Do you ever think about getting back together?"

There it was. The question that all kids asked divorced parents. It had not been asked of Jenny yet, as if the kids had known not to voice it, and Jenny was surprised that Alicia braved the question tonight.

A new rush of kids to the porch gave Jenny time to consider her answer, and when the final kid, a white-sheeted ghost, ran off, she said, "You do know how I feel about Steve."

Alicia nodded. "Like I feel about Tristen. Right? A boyfriend."

Jenny was glad the darkness could mask her smile. The way she felt about Steve was so much more than a middle school crush. She decided to circle around that last question. "Are you hoping that Daddy and I will get back together?"

Alicia shrugged.

"Be honest."

"Kinda."

The word was soft, barely audible, but Jenny didn't miss the emotion underneath it. "Okay. I'll be honest, too. And this may sting just a bit. But I'm not sure your father and I could ever remarry. I'm not even sure if I want to get married again. But if I do, it would be to Steve."

"But he's not our daddy."

Those words were harder. Stronger. And Jenny recognized the defiance that bolstered them.

That was a bit of a shock.

"I thought you liked Steve."

Alicia shrugged again.

"He wouldn't try to take the place of your father."

No response to that, and then they were interrupted by kids again. Jenny watched her daughter pass out candy, careful to note any signs of anxiety, but she appeared to be okay.

Long after the last trick or treaters had come and gone—those late-night teenagers who dressed up like hobos or their favorite sports figures and came with pillowcases already heavy with candy—Jenny sat on the porch thinking about the conversation with her daughter. Alicia had taken the pumpkin with the remnants of candy inside to watch the movie *Halloween*.

Before Alicia went inside, Jenny asked if she wanted to talk any more.

"Nope. I'm good."

"Turn off the porchlight."

"Okay."

Jenny smiled. It was like they hadn't had that very serious conversation. Trying to keep up with the mood swings of a teenage girl could give a person whiplash.

Not ready to go inside and watch television, Jenny sat in the inky darkness now that the porch light was out and puzzled over the questions Alicia had asked. What if she wasn't the only one that was hoping that Mom and Dad would get back together? Scott had never said anything about it, but then he knew more about the difficulties between her and Ralph when they were married. Maybe he'd long ago decided that together-again wasn't going to happen. But what if he secretly wanted it to?

For the first time since that wonderful night with Steve, Jenny started to wonder if trying to make a future with him was the best thing. In her heart, she knew it was the best thing for her. Oh, God, was it ever. But maybe not such a good thing for the kids? Should she just ask them outright?

First things first, she reminded herself. Let's see if anything happens with Steve beyond that one fabulous night.

Oh, please let something happen.

NINE

ANOTHER TWO AGONIZING weeks went by, and Jenny had heard precious little from Steve. He'd called a couple of times to tell her there were no leads yet on the burglar, and Jenny wanted to scream in frustration. In fact, she had screamed the one time he'd called her at the shop and Mitchell had given her a look that said, "You have got to tell me what that was about after you hang up."

A few minutes later, she did, and Mitchell gave her a hug before saying, "Why don't you take off early today? I can get the rest of the orders out."

"Are you sure?"

"Why is that the first thing someone asks after an offer like that?"

A smile accompanied the question, but Jenny did stop for a moment to consider why people did that. She shrugged. "Maybe an involuntary response?"

Mitchell nodded. "Probably so. And, yes, I am sure. So skedaddle."

Jenny laughed. Mitchell was the only person, besides her

mother, who could say skedaddle with a straight face. She went to her office and prepared a couple of invoices to send out to business clients who ordered fresh flowers from her on a weekly basis, and then she packed up and headed home, thankful to be earlier than her usual six or seven o'clock. Ralph was coming tonight to spend the weekend with the kids, so she'd have time to cook a real dinner before Scott had to head to the airport to pick up his father.

The first time Ralph had come just to visit, several months after Michael's funeral, he had rented a car at the airport, but when Scott got his license, he volunteered to pick his father up when he flew into town. Scott said he liked to play chauffeur for the weekend and save his dad some money. For her part, Jenny was happy that they had that extra time together. Fathers and sons needed all the time they could get.

Since Ralph had to work Thanksgiving week, this was going to be an early holiday celebration with the kids. Granted, it was going to be a short visit. He was coming in at eight tonight and leaving in the early evening on Sunday. That didn't allow for a lot of time together, but Jenny was grateful for whatever time Ralph had for the kids. They had been much happier these past two years, seeing him frequently, as opposed to those barren years when he had been so markedly absent.

Considering what Alicia had asked her, Jenny wondered if she should prepare a Thanksgiving dinner here tomorrow instead of them going out. She paused in her perusal of the refrigerator to consider that thought. The plan had been for Ralph to stay in a nearby motel, which he did every time he came to town. A plan arrived at by mutual agreement. The kids and Ralph had made arrangements to go to a movie tomorrow afternoon, and then they would have dinner at a restaurant. When he'd done that in the past, they all seemed to like it that way; the kids especially enjoying time alone with Dad. So? Should anything change just because?

Not to mention the fact that it is no easy feat to pull a Thanksgiving dinner together in twenty-four hours. Especially when some of those hours would be spent sleeping and a few more spent working. She only had a half-day at the shop tomorrow, but still. Wonder Woman in the kitchen she was not!

Jenny shook her head and closed the refrigerator. Nothing in there that could even pass for supper tonight. She grabbed her car keys and headed to the grocery store.

———

Early Saturday afternoon, Ralph came to meet up with the kids for the movie. He'd walked the few blocks from the motel, and his dark hair was tossed by the wind. He was wearing khaki slacks, a deep maroon polo shirt, and a wide smile. He gave Jenny a quick hug. "You're looking good."

A bit taken back, Jenny hesitated before responding, "Thanks."

"Are the kids ready?"

Jenny called up the staircase, "Your father's here."

Ralph leaned a shoulder against the wall in the entry. "You want to come to the show with us?"

That was also a surprise, and Jenny considered it for a moment and then shook her head. "I have to get back to the shop."

Before Ralph could respond, Scott came down the stairs and embraced his father in a hug that was all odd angles of arms and elbows that didn't seem to know where exactly to go. Jenny had to smile, recognizing the fact that they still needed a lot of practice with sharing affection.

Alicia came next, and she seemed more comfortable with the embrace.

"You guys ready to go?" Ralph asked.

Nods all around.

"What are you going to see?" Jenny asked.

"Something about school," Alicia said.

"Really? You don't get enough school in real life?"

Alicia chuckled. "It's a comedy. Real school isn't funny."

"It's *What I Learned in Middle School*," Scott said. "Or something like that."

Jenny looked at him, not able to keep the surprise off her face. "And you agreed to go?"

"Yeah. Gotta make the little sister happy sometimes."

Alicia punched Scott in the arm he grabbed his keys from the little dish on the table in the entryway and headed out the front door to his car.

"Have fun and be safe," Jenny called out.

Scott waved an acknowledgement, and Ralph hung back on the porch just a moment. "I've been trying to get the guts to ask you something."

"Not something horrid, I hope."

He shook his head, and then blurted, "Would you come to dinner with me and the kids tonight?"

Wow. Talk about a shock. "What about the time-alone-with-the-kids bit?"

His only answer was a shrug, so she asked, "Do they know about the invite?"

"Scott does. I mentioned it to him last night before he dropped me at the motel." He paused and glanced away.

"And?" she prompted.

Ralph cleared his throat then looked back at her. "He said it was up to you. He'd be cool either way."

Jenny smiled. So like Scott, always taking the middle ground.

"Hey, Dad," Scott called from the car. "You coming?"

"Don't answer now," Ralph said, his relief at the interruption evident on his face as he took a few steps away. "Let me know later. There's downtime between the movie and dinner reservations."

With that, he ran to the car and got in. Jenny stood on the porch, watching them drive off and shaking her head in disbelief. An old saying she'd heard her grandmother use came to mind. *Well, knock me over with a feather duster.*

————

Steve didn't always work on a Saturday, but this afternoon he hustled into the conference room where he saw Linda and the Chief waiting for him. Gonzales had called Steve when a girl, Yolanda, had walked into the station and said she knew who had been breaking into businesses downtown. Linda had talked to the girl long enough to determine she might be the real deal. You never knew. Crackpots came in all the time. Publicity seekers who wanted their sound bite on the evening news.

Steve thought she might be credible since Yolanda was the name Jenny had given him. Of course, he couldn't tell Gonzales that. He hadn't told anyone at the station about what Jenny had done or the tentative lead. He hadn't been able to find out anything about a Yolanda on his own, so he had let it drop. Now it looked like the lead might have dropped right back into his lap.

"Where is she?" Steve asked

They knew the "she" to whom he was referring. "Stashed in an interrogation room," Gonzales said. "Fredericks is keeping an eye on her."

"Think she's telling the truth?"

"Let's find out," Gonzales said, rising and heading to the door. "You and Linda talk to her. I'll watch."

Steve walked into the interrogation room and nodded at Fredericks to leave. Then Steve took a good look at the young woman seated at the dented metal table. Her complexion was dark, maybe black or Hispanic. Could be either with a name like Yolanda. Dark brown eyes bright with moisture looked back at him. Fingers tipped with bold red played with one of the hollows in the table. Steve remembered the fist that had created that hollow. It had belonged to a kid so high on meth he was one total jiggle from head to toe. The kid had taken umbrage to a question about where he had been when his mother and father had been killed and slammed his fist on the table. Pain hadn't even seemed to register, even when blood started seeping from splits in the skin on the guy's hand.

Steve smiled at Yolanda, to put her at ease, and then introduced himself and Linda before pulling a metal chair from the corner and sitting down across from her. He put the yellow legal pad and the ballpoint pen he'd brought with him on the table.

"So, Yolanda. You told my partner here that you know who is doing the downtown burglaries?"

He posed it as a question and she nodded.

"Can you give us the name?"

"First I need to know I won't be in trouble."

"Why would you be in trouble?" Linda asked from where she was leaning against the wall.

Yolanda looked over at Linda, then back to Steve. "He made me. You know. Help him at first."

"I see," Steve said, leaning back in his chair.

"But then I told him I didn't want to do it anymore."

"Do what?"

"You know. Break into the stores."

Steve nodded. "How many times did you go with him?"

"Twice."

"That's all?"

She nodded and then licked her lips. "Can I have some water?"

"Sure," Linda said, pushing away from the wall. "I'll get you some."

Steve didn't ask any more questions until Linda returned with a bottle of water which she slid across the table to Yolanda.

"Okay," Steve said when Linda took her position at the wall again. He slid the legal pad toward Yolanda. "Write down this boyfriend's name."

"You didn't say whether I'd be in trouble."

"I won't lie to you," Steve said. "This doesn't work like it does on TV. There are no guarantees. But I will speak to the DA. Let her know you're cooperating."

Yolanda took a long swallow of the water. "He's gonna be pissed. I don't know what he'll do."

"Is he violent?" Linda asked.

"Sometimes." Yolanda dipped her chin and looked at the table. "He can be a mean drunk."

Steve leaned over the table until he was sure he was in her line of sight and didn't speak until she looked up again. "He can't hurt you if we have him locked up."

"What about until then?" It was a soft, whispered question.

"You got family? Friends you could stay with?"

She shook her head. "Family is all back east. And he knows my friends. He'd know where to look for me if I wasn't home."

Steve waited another long moment before he said, "Then I guess we shouldn't waste any more time here."

He pushed the tablet even closer to her, and she awkwardly picked up the pen and started writing.

"Put down where we can find him," Steve said. "The two of you living together?"

She shook her head. "He's crashing with a buddy. I kicked him out when he went back on the drugs. I worked too hard to get clean to let him mess me up again."

That revelation came as a bit of a surprise. Steve had thought the wide-eyed look was from her being high, but he had to reconsider. Either she was lying about being clean, or his cop radar was on the fritz.

"You did rehab?"

Yolanda nodded. "And got a job. Not a great one, but a job. Pays enough for rent."

Linda came over and leaned a hip on the table. "Then why'd you agree to help him with the burglaries?"

An expressive shrug was the first response. Then Yolanda said, "Enrique promised we'd just do it a couple of times. Get enough money for him to go into rehab. Then when he was clean, we'd get married. Handed me a great big line of shit."

"That's all some guys know how to dish out," Linda said.

"You're doing the right thing," Steve said. "Talking to us like this."

Steve waited a moment to let her digest that, then asked, "Do you know an address for the buddy Enrique might be with?"

Yolanda shook her head. "He wouldn't tell me. But he's supposed to come by at nine tonight. For one last job, he said. Bullshit. That's what he said after the second time, and the third."

Linda jumped on the contradiction. "But you said you only did two burglaries with him."

"That's right. But he still came over to brag on what he got from the others. When I told him I didn't care, he just laughed. Asked did I forget about our plans. Shit. There ain't ever going to be just one last job."

"Yes, there is," Steve said. "The last one was the last one."

The briefest of smiles touched Yolanda lips.

TEN

BEFORE RALPH and the kids returned from the theater, Jenny had decided that she would accept his invitation to join them for dinner. That is, if the kids seemed eager to have her. Knowing that Ralph had made reservations at The Loft, one of the nicer places in town, she dressed in a long black skirt and white lacy blouse, with her mother's gray pearls around her neck. It just felt like the kind of outfit a mother should wear to go to dinner with her kids, and conservative seemed like a good choice for dining with an ex-husband.

She was downstairs in the living room, reading a book, when Ralph and the kids burst through the door. They were smiling and talking over each other as they came into the house, and they all stopped dead when they saw her. "Mom," Alicia said. "You look so pretty."

Jenny closed the book. "Thanks."

"You going out?" Scott asked.

Before Jenny could answer, Ralph spoke. "You decided to come with us."

It wasn't a question, but Jenny still nodded. Alicia squealed and hugged her. "It will be such fun."

Since Scott's Honda had such a small back seat, Jenny offered to drive to the restaurant. It was on the edge of town in an old barn, not the sort of setting for an upscale restaurant. But the young couple who had purchased the McDougal place had created quite a masterpiece inside and out. A large mural graced one side of the barn, which had been re-painted with the traditional red color before the art was added. Jenny always stopped a moment to appreciate the scene depicted on the side of the barn, wondering if the farmer walking through a meadow with a child in tow was old Mr. McDougal. The older couple had four children and a passel of grandchildren, and word was they had gone to live with the daughter in Colorado after selling the home place to Brad and Tina.

Inside, the barn had been transformed into a fine-dining establishment with linen and crystal on the tables. True to its name, there was seating in the former hayloft, which is where the hostess took Jenny and the family. Downstairs, the once open space had been divided into several rooms for intimate dining, and abstract paintings decorated most of the walls. There wasn't a saddle or a spur or a piece of barbed wire in sight.

The menu tonight included some of the standard Thanksgiving dinner items, but there was also a choice of steaks, prime rib, and Cornish hen.

They all opted for the turkey and all the trimmings. Some habits are hard to break.

After the meal was served and they started eating, Jenny noticed a great disparity between the kids. Scott ate quietly, not giving any indication of whether he was comfortable having dinner with Mom and Dad, but Alicia bubbled over with talk about school, the movie, and anything else that popped into her head. Jenny listened and nodded and um-hummed in all the right places, a bit surprised at how comfortable it was. At times Alicia was quiet, focusing on her dinner, but Jenny didn't miss the meaning in the looks her daughter gave her. *Isn't this nice? We can be a family.*

Jenny didn't respond to the glances, pretending she was oblivious, but she wondered what had happened to that teenage girl who was all over Steve like melting butter just a couple of weeks ago. That same teenage girl who had appeared so excited that Steve had come back into their lives.

What had changed?

Jenny glanced over at Ralph, who was smiling broadly at Alicia.

Of course. That's what had changed.

And she had to admit this evening had been nice. The meal had not been on par with the traditional Thanksgiving dinners her mother prepared, but it had been tasty, and Jenny was savoring the last bites of pumpkin pie, thinking how different Ralph was now from the man she'd walked away from eight years ago. All through dinner, he'd been attentive to her and to the kids, and a bit of that man she had once loved had been shining through. *Oh my gosh. Am I really having romantic thoughts about my ex?*

The mental question made her smile, and Ralph smiled back. Jenny quickly looked away, taking the last bite of her pie. *Don't give him any reason to think the smile meant anything.*

———

Steve slowed the unmarked car a few doors from the address that Yolanda had given them. It was 8:30. Almost a half-hour to wait, and the street was dark. The corner light had blown out, and they had only passed a few homes that had light spilling out of windows. In contrast, Yolanda's house looked like it was lit up for Christmas.

"Geez. Will you look at that," Linda said. "Think she always has so many lights on?"

"Hope so." Steve pulled to the curb and doused the lights. "Don't want something different to spook him."

"Think he'll show?"

Steve shrugged.

"If you just answered with a shrug, I can't see that in the dark."

Steve gave a soft laugh.

"How will we play this?" Linda asked. "Wait for him to go inside?"

"No. Too dangerous for Yolanda. Soon as he pulls up in that old Camaro she described, we take him down."

Forty minutes later a dusty gray Camaro with dented, rusting rocker panels rolled slowly down the street, passed the unmarked car, and idled in front of Yolanda's house.

Linda reached for the door handle on her side of the car, and Steve put a hand on her arm. "Wait."

Steve figured Enrique was too smart to just park and go in on first pass, and sure enough, the Camaro sped off. A few minutes later, it approached from the other direction, and this time the car stopped in front of a house opposite Yolanda's.

The officers waited until Enrique had come out of the car, walking resolutely across the street, before slipping out of their car. Steve had dismantled the interior roof light earlier, so nothing would alert the kid. He and Linda moved quickly but silently on soft-soled shoes, along the street, gaining on Enrique.

Then suddenly Enrique glanced back. Saw the cops. And ran. Straight into the house. The door banging shut after him.

"Shit!" Steve slid to a stop on the front step.

"Now what?" Linda whispered beside him.

"Call for backup. Then go around to the rear. I'll see if I can talk him out."

———

Once back at home, Jenny kicked off her high heels and sank to the sofa, rubbing her sore feet. It had been ages since she'd worn heels and her feet were not happy. Ralph stood there, looking a bit uncertain, so she asked if he'd like to stay for coffee. No way was she going to offer anything else to drink. Offering wine or a mixed drink might give an impression she didn't want to make—the last scene of the perfect date.

"Sure. Coffee would be great," Ralph said.

Jenny went to the kitchen to get the coffee brewing, and the kids each grabbed bottled water out of the refrigerator before joining their father in the living room.

A couple of minutes later, Jenny paused in the doorway to the living room. "I'm going upstairs to change. Be right back."

When the coffee was served, they all sat in the living room, talking about plans for Christmas. The kids would be flying to California for the holidays, and details were ironed out as to flight schedules, who would be responsible for letting Jenny know they had landed safely, and what day they would return.

Once that was all settled, Ralph drained the last of his coffee and looked at Jenny. "Could you drop me at the motel?"

That request took Jenny by surprise. What could he want? "I thought Scott was going to do that."

"Could you? There's something we need to talk about."

What on earth could that be? Jenny quickly dismissed the inkling of an idea that first popped into her head, realizing that he probably wanted to talk about presents for the kids. They couldn't discuss that in front of them after all. "Is that okay with you kids?" Jenny asked.

"Sure," Scott said. "Then I can call Caitlin before it is too late."

Alicia didn't say anything, but her smile spoke volumes.

"Okay, then." Jenny stood and went to the hall table to get her purse. "You ready?"

"Sure." Ralph hugged the kids each in turn, then followed Jenny out.

During the short drive to the motel, into the glow of streetlights and then into darkness again, Jenny wondered when Ralph was going to get around to saying what he wanted to. As it turned out, he waited until she pulled into the parking lot by the front entrance. "You want to come in?"

She shook her head. After what she'd been thinking at dinner, she figured going into the motel with him would not be a good idea, even if he only meant to the lobby. She rolled down her window and let the cool evening breeze blow in.

It took another long minute before Ralph spoke again. "When I'm with the kids now, it feels good. Like it used to be."

Jenny bit back a sharp retort. What "used to be"? It never had been good. Did he forget all those years when they were a family minus one? All the years he'd been too busy with work, or whatever, to be home for dinner. Or go on a family picnic. Or come to Michael's football games?

Granted, he was now trying his best to be a caring father to the kids. And recently, she'd worked hard to forget all the ways he'd hurt her, and them, but forgetting wasn't very easy.

Ralph seemed to sense her thoughts. "I know it wasn't great when the kids were little. I was a rotten father. But lately. Since ..."

He struggled to finish, but Jenny knew what he couldn't say, so she did. "Since Michael."

"Yes." Ralph took a deep breath. "We've all been getting along so much better, I thought maybe it could work with us again." He shrugged. "Maybe we could make this a real family again."

Once more, Jenny had to stifle the urge to remind him there was no "again" about it. She bit her lip for a moment, then said, "Have you talked to the kids about that?"

"Not a lot. You know me."

Jenny smiled. Yes, she did know him. A man of few words if those words involved feelings. "Did they have anything to say about the idea?"

"Yeah. Yeah, they did." Ralph's voice held a note of excitement. "Alicia said it would be cool."

"What about Scott?"

"He said he wouldn't mind."

Now Jenny laughed. So like Scott. Don't commit until you know what the other person is going to do. She studied Ralph's face which was indistinct in the night shadows, but she always had a clear mental image of his face, so handsome at times it could turn heads, and often did. She sighed. "I'm going to have to think about this."

"Of course. I understand."

Silence again for a moment, and then she said, "You have to know I have feelings for Steve."

"Yes. I know." He took a breath. "But you once had feelings for me."

Jenny nodded. A tangle of emotions choked her, and she couldn't speak.

"Don't answer until you are sure. Just think about it."

With that, he got out of the car and pushed the door closed with a soft click. She watched through the windshield as he walked to the motel entrance in quick strides, holding himself ramrod straight. He didn't look back.

Driving home, Jenny played the last few minutes through her mind, trying to make sense of it all. Why did Ralph have to make this request of her now? A year ago, the answer might have been so much clearer.

It might have even been, "Yes." The pull to unite the family had been stronger then.

Now, she wasn't sure. Well, actually she was sure. Even this new kinder Ralph did not make her heart swell the way it did with Steve. The only reason she would even consider saying yes to Ralph now would be for the kids. But was that good enough? Was that fair to any of them?

ELEVEN

STEVE POUNDED on the closed door, calling out, "Open up, Enrique. Let's end this with both of us standing."

No response.

Shit.

"Come on, man. At least let your girl go."

From inside, Steve heard the hard slap of flesh against flesh, and then a scream and a loud thump. "She ain't going nowhere," a voice called out.

Shit.

After a few moments, Enrique called out, "Did she rat me out?"

"No." Steve mentally scrambled for something to avert the man's suspicions. "Your car was IDed."

Nothing else from inside the house, so Steve said, "Don't add to your troubles, man. Let her go."

Silence.

Steve had been concentrating so completely on his efforts to talk Enrique into giving up, he had not been aware of the two patrol cars that had pulled up in front of the house. They had come in silent.

"Steve," said a voice to his right, and Steve turned to see Gonzales.

"What's the status?" the Chief asked.

Steve quickly brought the Chief up to speed, and then they heard a loud scream from inside. High-pitched. A woman. Gonzales turned to a patrol officer who was standing just behind him with a battering ram. "Open it up."

The officer blasted them through the door and into the living room. Steve could make out the figure of Yolanda on the floor. He also saw the shadow of a man moving through a doorway that probably led to a kitchen in the back.

Torn between following the suspect and checking on the woman, Steve hesitated for just a beat. "Go," Gonzales called out. "I've got this."

Steve nodded and ran toward the opening to the other room. There, he saw the back door wide open and heard the scrabbling sounds of a struggle from outside. Following the sounds, he quickly ran into the backyard. Linda was on the ground, wrestling with Enrique, both of them rolling through bare, dusty patches of dirt in what was supposed to be a lawn. Arms and legs and fists tangled together, and it was hard to tell who had the upper hand.

"A little help here," Linda gasped when Enrique pinned her, hands around her throat.

Steve grabbed the man by his shoulders and pulled him off Linda, throwing him roughly to the ground. He put his foot on Enrique's back. "Give me a reason to break a few ribs."

The man didn't move.

Linda rolled to her knees, then pulled herself upright, rubbing her throat gingerly. She watched as Steve handcuffed the man, then jerked him to his feet.

Enrique shot a wad of spit in Steve's face.

"You shouldn't have done that," Linda said to Enrique as Steve raised a foot and kicked the man with such force he fell with a loud thump.

Linda grabbed Steve's arm and pulled him away just as Gonzales stepped out of the house. "What's going on here?"

"Just subduing a suspect, Chief." Steve twisted out of Linda's grasp and jerked Enrique to his feet again.

"I see that." The chief refrained from saying he hoped the suspect didn't press charges for police brutality, and Steve knew it was only because the chief didn't want to give the man any ideas.

"I'll take him," Linda said, grabbing Enrique and moving him toward the door to the house.

"If he blinks wrong, kick him in the nuts," Steve called out.

"Hey, man. I got rights."

"Yeah. The only right you have is the right to get your ass kicked."

"Get him out of here," Gonzales said to Linda. Then he turned to Steve. "We're not on the school playground anymore."

"I know." Steve adjusted his shirt that had come untucked in the tussle. "Just severely pissed at what he did to the girl. How is she?"

"She's alive. Barely. The ass-wipe did a number on her. Ambulance is on the way."

The distant whine of sirens slowly grew louder as the men went back into the house. A patrol officer was hunched near Yolanda, who was still sprawled on the floor. "Is she conscious?" Steve asked stepping up beside the officer.

Reynolds shook his head. "But she's still breathing."

"Breathing is good," Steve said.

"She's got a nasty wound on her head," Reynolds said. "I

think it was caused by that."

He pointed to a trophy that had blood on the base, and Steve stepped over for a closer look. It was a soccer trophy. The figure on top was female, so Steve surmised that at one time Yolanda might have played the sport. She appeared to be too young to have a daughter old enough to be on a senior team.

The sirens screamed louder, then came to a sudden stop. The silence was deafening. Then two male paramedics charged through the open front door, bags of medical items thrown across broad shoulders. Steve and Reynolds stepped away from Yolanda, giving the EMTs room to work, which they did quickly and efficiently, all the while reporting to the ER nurse at the hospital.

Steve knew the routine from too many other scenes just like this one, so he stayed by the fireplace and remained quiet, but he was alert to every movement and every bit of the reports. "Pulse thready. Respirations slow."

Once the paramedics had an IV line working, one went out and got a stretcher to transport Yolanda.

"Where you taking her?" Steve asked.

"County," the other man said as his partner came back with the stretcher. They quickly strapped Yolanda in, ready to wheel her out.

"I'll come along," Steve said.

"Suit yourself."

Steve hustled after the EMTs, pausing just long enough to tell Gonzales he was riding in the ambulance to the hospital.

"What the hell for?"

Steve shrugged. "Don't want to sit at my place waiting to hear if she makes it."

"How you gonna get home?"

"I'll figure something out."

"Who'll fill out the report?"

"Linda tackled the guy. It's her collar."

Gonzales snorted as Steve made a mad dash to the ambulance just as the rear doors were about to close.

Three hours later the transportation Steve figured out was a call to the station to see who was on night patrol. Turned out Reynolds could give him a ride from the hospital to his apartment. Since there was the small matter of a policy against using patrol as a taxi service, Gonzales would not be thrilled. But what the hell. Steve had done worse and not been canned.

The latest report on Yolanda from the doctor was guarded, but hopeful. She had a severe concussion, but the doctor said that, in a way, she had been lucky to have an open wound. Saved her from an internal bleed. A couple of ribs were broken, and she had other contusions on her upper body, neck, and head. She was still unconscious, which wasn't a good thing. But if she woke up in the next twenty-four or forty-eight hours, that *would* be a good thing.

That last had been an understatement if Steve ever heard one. But he'd been relieved to hear the girl was still alive. As long as she was still breathing, she had a chance.

Before he left the hospital, he pulled out his cell phone and dialed Jenny's number. She was the only person he felt like talking to tonight. She answered on the fifth ring, her voice a bit muffled. He glanced at the clock in the waiting room. Crap! It was almost midnight.

"Sorry. Didn't mean to wake you," he said, feeling stupid for even saying that.

"Who is this?"

Briefly, Steve wondered at the wisdom of just hanging up. If she didn't know who it was, it could remain a mystery. But he didn't want to hang up. "Steve."

"Oh. You were talking so low, I didn't recognize your voice. Is anything wrong?"

"No. No. I'm at the hospital."

"What?"

That question came with the force of a sonic blast, and he quickly tried to put her at ease. "It's okay. I'm okay."

"Then what are you doing at the hospital?"

"That girl you told me about a couple of weeks ago. Yolanda?"

"Yes."

"She was badly injured."

"Oh my God! What happened?"

Steve gave her the condensed version of events from the time Yolanda first came to the station up through tonight, finishing with, "The last time that dirtbag hit her, he used more than just his fist. She has a pretty bad concussion."

There was no response for several long moments, so Steve said, "You still there?"

A "yes" rode on a deep sigh, then Jenny continued. "I feel so bad. I should never have gotten her involved."

"Yolanda was already involved. And she came to us on her own. She didn't even mention talking to your little friend."

"Is that supposed to make me feel better?"

Steve wiped a hand across his face. "I hope so."

There was silence again for a few moments before Steve asked, "Listen. Do you think we can meet somewhere? Have coffee?"

"Now?"

"Yeah."

"Where?"

"I think Denny's is the only place open."

"Really? Denny's? I haven't been there in—"

"Please?"

Another deep sigh, and then, "Okay. Give me thirty minutes."

TWELVE

JENNY PUT the phone down on her nightstand and slipped out of bed. Quietly, she got some jeans and a shirt from her closet and dressed. She didn't have to think about what to wear to Denny's. It didn't even have to be casual-chic, so she just grabbed the first shirt her fingers touched. Then she put on sneakers, grabbed her phone, and tip-toed out. Just in case one of the kids woke up while she was gone, she left a note on the kitchen table:

Gone out for coffee. Be back by one.

Love, Mom

If they woke and saw the note, she'd explain it all later.

She put her car in neutral and let it roll out of the drive, taking advantage of the incline, and had to chuckle. The maneuvering to get out without being noticed took her back to her teenage years, sneaking out of her parent's house.

The giddiness, whether from her memories or the lack of sleep, stayed with Jenny until she got to the restaurant and spotted Steve in a booth near the back. The place was nearly empty. A booth at the front had three young people in it, and a couple that could have been husband and wife sat in another. A heavyset man sat at the counter, and he turned to look at Jenny as she stepped in. He gave her a lopsided grin and said, "Lookin' for company, pretty girl?"

The words were slurred, and Jenny ignored him, picking up her steps as she walked toward the far booth.

"Didn't mean nothin'," the man muttered as she hurried past.

"Now I know why I don't like to come here," Jenny said as she sat down, noting that Steve had a steaming mug of coffee in front of him, seemingly untouched.

"He's harmless," Steve said, nodding toward the man at the counter. "The waitress said he comes in every night. Doesn't bother anyone if they don't want to be bothered."

The waitress, an older woman with a tired expression and a little too much makeup, came over with an empty cup in one hand and a coffeepot in the other. "Coffee for you, ma'am?"

"Yes. Thank you."

The woman poured the steaming liquid into the heavy white mug, then walked away. Jenny put some cream and sugar in, hoping that would cut the acid and save her stomach. As she stirred, she took a close look at Steve. "You okay?"

He didn't answer for a moment, so she pushed. It hurt to see the lines of distress on his face. "Come on, Steve. Talk to me."

He gave a little shake of his head as if trying to get rid of unwanted thoughts. "I should have moved faster. Gotten that bastard before he could get into the house."

"Didn't you tell me that what other people choose to do is not our fault? I seem to remember those words from two years ago. Doesn't that apply now? To you. To what happened tonight?"

"Yeah. Right." The words were those of agreement, but the tone was a contradiction.

Jenny studied the set of his jaw, the muscle twitching in his cheek, considering how to respond. Challenge him, or come at him soft and easy? In her months of counseling after the killing two years ago, she'd learned one thing. Don't beat yourself up over something you had no control over. Kind of went along with the Serenity Prayer that her therapist told her to tape to her bathroom mirror.

It worked.

Not always and not right away, but in time, Jenny had let go of some of her feelings of responsibility for Michael and for everything that had followed.

So that's what she said to Steve. "Don't beat yourself up over something you had no control over."

Steve wiped a hand across his face. "What if she dies?"

"Don't. Don't play the 'what if' game. She's alive. She'll pull out of this."

Steve sat for the longest time, not saying anything. Not looking at her. Then he took a hefty swallow of coffee, set the mug back down, and said. "Coffee tastes terrible when it's cold."

Jenny smiled and motioned to the waitress who understood the traditional signal and came over with a fresh pot, refilling both mugs. After she left, Steve looked over at Jenny, raising his mug in a mock toast. "Thanks."

"For?"

"Agreeing to meet me. Talking. Making me feel better."

"You're welcome."

The waitress came back to see if they wanted anything else, and Jenny asked if there was any pie. She needed something on her stomach besides this strong coffee.

"We have one piece of apple left, and two of chocolate meringue."

"I'll take the apple," Jenny said, then looked at Steve. "You want anything?"

Steve looked at the waitress. "Got any carrot cake?"

"Sure do."

"Okay."

After the waitress moved away, Jenny chuckled. "Took us long enough to get dessert."

"Huh?"

"The hotel?" Jenny grinned. "We never ..."

"Oh. Right."

Now Steve grinned and abruptly asked, "Can I kiss you?"

"Right here in front of God and that drunk at the counter?"

Steve chuckled. "Yes. In front of everyone."

Jenny nodded, thinking he would simply lean across and give her a chaste peck on the cheek, but he stood, pulling her to her feet and kissing her soundly before calling out, "Hey, everyone. This is the woman I love."

"Steve! Everyone is staring."

"I don't care." Steve called out to the room at large again, "This is the woman I want to marry. Anybody got a ring?"

The drunk peeled away from the counter and staggered over. He reached into his shirt pocket and extracted a cigar, pulling off the paper ring and holding it out to Steve. "Will this do?"

"Yes." Steve took the flimsy paper and turned back to Jenny.

"But I didn't say yes," she protested.

"Now is your chance." Steve got down on one knee, holding the ring aloft. "Jenny Jasik, will you please marry me and make my life complete?"

Jenny's heart thumped so hard in her chest, she thought it

might burst right out. Now she knew for sure what she would say in answer to Ralph's earlier question. All her life she'd made decisions for the kids. For Ralph. For other people. Now it was time to make a decision for herself.

She held out her hand. "Yes, Steve. I'll marry you."

As Steve slipped the paper ring on the appropriate finger of her left hand, the sparse crowd in the diner all stood and applauded. Then Steve kissed her again, a slow, languid kiss that set her afire.

The waitress stepped up. "You two still want dessert?"

Jenny pulled back and laughed. "Oh yes. We always want dessert."

THE END

Dear reader,

We hope you enjoyed reading *One Perfect Love*. Please take a moment to leave a review, even if it's a short one. Your opinion is important to us.

Discover more books by Maryann Miller at

https://www.nextchapter.pub/authors/maryann-miller

Want to know when one of our books is free or discounted? Join the newsletter at

http://eepurl.com/bqqB3H

Best regards,

Maryann Miller and the Next Chapter Team

You might also like:
Evelyn Evolving by Maryann Miller

To read the first chapter for free, head to:
https://www.nextchapter.pub/books/evelyn-evolving

ABOUT THE AUTHOR

Maryann Miller is an award-winning author of numerous books, screenplays, and stage plays. She started her professional career as a journalist, writing columns, feature stories, and short fiction for regional and national publications. A sequel to *One Small Victory*, *One Perfect Love* is Miller's third book to be published by Next Chapter. *Evelyn Evolving: A Story of Real Life*, was released in May 2019 and celebrates the strength of her mother's life.

In addition to women's novels and short stories, she has written a number of mysteries, including the critically-acclaimed Seasons Mystery Series that features two women homicide detectives. Think *Lethal Weapon* set in Dallas with female leads. The first two books in the series, *Open Season* and *Stalking Season* have received starred reviews from Publisher's Weekly, Kirkus, and Library Journal. *Stalking Season* was chosen for the John E. Weaver Excellence in Reading award for Police Procedural Mysteries.

Other awards Miller has received for her writing are the Page Edwards Short Story Award, the New York Library Best Books for Teens Award, first place in the screenwriting competition at the Houston Writer's Conference, placing as a semi-finalist at Sundance, and placing as a semi-finalist in the Chesterfield Screenwriting Competition. She was named The Trails Country Treasure by the Winnsboro Center for the Arts, and Woman of the Year in by the Winnsboro Area Chamber of Commerce.

Miller can be found at her Amazon Author Page her Website on Twitter and Facebook and Goodreads She is a contributor to The Blood-Red Pencil blog on writing and editing.

When not writing, Maryann likes to play on stage and was the Theatre Director at the Winnsboro Center for the Arts for fifteen years, where she ran the annual Youth Drama Camp. She can die happy now that she has played one of her favorite roles as Martha in "Arsenic and Old Lace."

A Note from the Author

First, thank you so much for purchasing my book and reading it. I do hope you enjoyed the story, and I would appreciate it if you could take a moment to rate and review it at Amazon and at Goodreads. Reviews can do so much to help authors get exposure and gain new readers.

Happy Reading!

Maryann

One Perfect Love
ISBN: 978-4-86750-077-4

Published by
Next Chapter
1-60-20 Minami-Otsuka
170-0005 Toshima-Ku, Tokyo
+818035793528

4th June 2021